N.C. 7.

Not so good

DULL

TOO FAR TO WALK

TOO FAR
TO WALK

John Hersey

New York Alfred·A·Knopf

1966

c2

L. C. catalog card number: 66–13500

THIS IS A BORZOI BOOK,
PUBLISHED BY ALFRED A. KNOPF, INC.

FIRST EDITION

BOOK ONE

I

THEY were speeding along the new throughway down the valley at three in the morning under a wet full moon. Breed drove, hunched over, steering with a wary grip as if the wheel itself were a ring of sleep. John Fist sat in back, on the right, watching the long wrapper-tobacco barns float past, which he knew to be red by day, but were black now in the silver night mist, their red pigment lying in wait against the wood for another day's illusions.

The four had given up talking. For the first few miles they had raked over the girls at the stupid mixer. John felt cold. The engine, behind him, had a high alien whine.

On the right, a wooded rise, some hemlocks running in a pack, dark gowns flying; then the shapes were gone. . . .

3

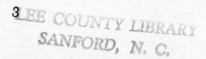

For a time John shut his eyes, and on the screen of his lids he made out a glow, like an afterimage of the sort that would come when he rubbed his eyes and kept them closed—was it face-shaped? The girl at the dance in a black turtleneck and coral necklace, with a voice all hints, offers, fugues? Her parents had given her an acetylene torch for her birthday, and she said she was going to make metal constructions "like you never saw." Her hands were a pair of Vise-Grip wrenches, real rod-benders. *Idiocy* to go so far for a lousy affair like that in the middle of the week. They had been spurred by a dare of Breed's.

John shivered. The vague luster had faded from his eyes, and he opened them to another radiance, up front, over Wagner's shoulder: the needle trembling on the rind of numbers, at seventy.

Breed was way over in the leftmost of the three lanes, and he had that little sewing machine of an engine really stitching. He wasn't even supposed to keep a car at college; it was in somebody else's name, a senior's name, but it was Breed's.

They flew past toll signs, Breed down-shifted, the car crept toward the single open slot in the toll gates. A VW bus, ahead of them, stood in the chute the longest time. At last it started away, and Breed pulled his car forward, rolling down the window on his side.

Wagner, handing Breed change, said: —— Here, Chum.

As Breed reached out to the tollgatherer, Wagner sat up straight: —— Hey, look at that hombre.

The VW bus, gaining speed, had seemed to lurch from one lane to another. Now an oversteadying hand swerved it more than back.

—— That boy is really sloshed.

4

Gibbon, beside John: —— Don't pass him, Breed.

Breed was soon up to sixty; he stayed close behind the bus, which veered again.

Wagner said: —— Wild.

Gibbon, tensely leaning forward: —— Come on, Breed, don't tailgate the son of a bitch.

Breed said it would take all night this way, but he let some space open up. Not that he slowed down—the VW was going faster.

Up ahead John could see the string of lights of a service center, and against their glare the little bus seemed to be coursing like a frantic dog on the hunt for some wavering quarry. The boxlike shape, bounding forward, would suddenly sheer to one side, until at last the driver's sluggish reflexes would pull it back, just in time, it seemed. Breed chafed but gave plenty of room, more than a hundred yards now.

Gibbon, both hands on the front seats: —— I can't watch. (But he did.)

They came up under the arching lights. Just there the bus, on the right lane, yawed once more and headed on a crazy angle to the left.

Wagner, the athlete, sharply, as if to wake the man up: —— Watch it!

The wheels of the bus hung a moment at the edge of the left lane, then, at more than sixty-five, they moved onto the dirt of the wide center strip, throwing up a thin dust into the showering candlepower of the high lamps. John had time to see that there was an anti-pedestrian chain-wire fence along this stretch of the grass divider. The bus went into the beginning of a big skid toward the fence, began to bounce, tripped, rolled over twice, burst through to the other side as though the fence were made of paper, stood up catlike on its wheels on the opposite

5

lanes in the lights of an oncoming car, and coasted gently to a stop. The door opened. The driver stepped sedately out as if he had reached his destination in a normal way, began to run flapping toward the gas station on the far side, and then, washed with light, fell on the pavement. There was a long shriek of skidding tires. John couldn't see out the small back window what happened.

Wagner: —— Holy cow, Breed, aren't you going to stop?

Breed: —— I have an eight-ten in the morning.

John: —— Brother.

But that was all John said or did.

2

He put out a hand to cut the alarm. Then he pulled the covers all the way up over his head, and he floated in the sac of his own warmth.

At some point he realized that he had decided to cut Orreman's nine-ten lecture; he might never go to Orreman's class again. Flooded with a delicious sense of relief, he shifted position under the covers.

Almost at once he stirred more restlessly, having begun to feel a bruise on his consciousness—the accident of the night before. Something made him think of steak. The old mother-remedy, press a beefsteak on a mouse?

He remembered then that he and his friends had not had time for any dinner driving up to Greenway, and he had skipped lunch the day before, too; the last he had eaten had been a glazed doughnut and a cup of coffee after his first class the previous morning.

Next he was standing in the center of the room, a belt of hunger tight at his waist. He swayed. Flack was up and gone, his bed ferociously unmade. Flack was tidier than John, and perhaps this was what made the rumpled bed so annoying now. The whole floor was a clutter beyond John's belief, and most of the mess was his own: *his* dirty underwear and socks, *his* slacks, loafers, sweaters, jackets, strewn on the rug, dripping from chairs. Not that Flack was all that fastidious. Flack's can opener, dangerous to bare feet, in the middle of the floor, Flack's incredible squash racket, Flack's record albums: "Ella Sings Gershwin," a Getz-Gilberto anthology. Right at John's feet (his toes seemed to him to be pale, bloodless, thin, and greatly distant) lay a two-day-old *New York Times:* Tshombe flies to Paris to seek backing, Vietcong ambush kills seven Americans.

There was still time to make Orreman's lecture, but John knew he was not going. Along with the hunger there was a knot of elation, at the solar-plexal seat of some sort of pleasant opening-up in him.

John Fist stood just under six feet in pajama pants and T-shirt, shivering in a momentary pause of indecision. He saw in his chiffonier mirror: a *young* face. He frowned. Did a somber look give him any seniority? His light-brown hair, slightly curly, was negligently full at ears and nape and now also hung in a loose twist over his forehead. He flapped it back with a hand that might have been going up in a military salute, and he moved with a slight stagger of his slow-starting energies to his dresser and banged the upper-right drawer with the heel of this same hand. Sheldon College made a big ado about a forty-one-thousand-dollar endowment standing behind each undergraduate, but the shitty drawers stuck. Shaking the whole chest, he worked the drawer open, only to find no undershorts left.

He groaned. He stooped to pick over some of the clothes on the floor. With a sudden burst he threw a few things on the foot of his bed, intending to do, then and there, a fantastic cleanup job. He felt very angry with Flack. The tidying impulse quickly spent itself, and he dropped onto the straight chair at his desk.

John had just about had Flack. Metlin T. Flack was one of those characters who seem perfectly fascinating for about two weeks in the spring term of freshman year, and John had signed up to room with him during that bughouse fortnight. Flack was a geographic-distribution beneficiary—from a high school in Helena, Montana, a test-passer, a knobby, innocent boy, as hardy and humble as bunch grass, son of a Pontiac dealer, descendant of sheep-raisers and of missionaries who had settled at Last Chance Gulch in the gold days. Would have gone to Carroll College, right at home, but had had a brainstorm and applied to Sheldon with his eyes closed, and had got in. As a freshman he had been rather bewildered, and had had to struggle to keep up with his courses; and he had seemed to flower in struggle. But now as a sophomore he had suddenly gone Deke, Ivy, Eastern. Flack now had a closetful of charcoal, Oxford, hopsack, classic, Glen, dripdry. Flack now played squash, the gentleman's sport. Flack in the shower sounded like a surfacing porpoise. Would wind up as a big personnel executive or something in a big detergent manufactorium or something; you could hear his efficient mind click as a pine borer clicks, at more or less regular intervals. Breed despised him.

John surveyed the heap on his desk. What a drift of

paperbacks, postponements, sore points of incompletion in longhand draft, far too much reading, indigestible assignments (*Daedalus:* "A New Europe?"), signs of straying from the pressure path (*Playboy, Evergreen Review:* "The Hair-Despoiling Perversion in Classical Literature"), records not returned to their albums, doodles, notes, scraps, addresses, snapshots.

Underneath, in the way of his feet, lay a mover's carton of books; he and Flack had planned at the beginning of the year to get some bricks and boards and make shelves.

His eye fell on some unopened letters. The big thing was not to open mail. Let it ripen. John never knew whether to laugh or throw up at the sight of the guys in the college post office, bent over, twirling the combinations on their boxes, pulling out letters, and, still stooped down, snatching at the flaps like famished crows pecking at carrion.

Idly John picked up and turned over in his hand a special-delivery. Maybe it would be O.K. to open a special-delivery letter—might have a check in it, though there was no particular reason to think it should; it must be a couple of weeks old by now, anyhow. He slit the envelope with a ball-point pen.

My darling Johnnycake:

Just a note to tell you we finally had to put poor dear old Ptolemy away. Dr. Vinton said his other eye was about to go, and his arthritis was so bad. Your father says Ptolemy was solid gold, about five thousand in vet's bills alone, but I say he was worth every cent of it—just to see him in bed with you, the way he used to nibble at you though he could have eaten you alive, goodness, my big Sheldon sophomore, that was nine-ten years ago, you couldn't have been more than a fifth-grader or so. You and Ptolemy were about the same size. And to see you two walk down the hill together toward the Parminters' in the snow. Blue parka, black dog—I can see it now! Funny the way he chose you. Never had much to do with either Siever or Lisa, did he. You had such a loving nature.

Well the annual trip. I think we will go to a place called Virgin Gorda, it's in the British Virgin Islands. They say there's a hat full of flying, San Juan then change planes to Saint Thomas then a tiny private thing to a spit of land and a boat trip on top of that. Your father wanted to try Mexico City but I feel he should go really tropical. He gets so used up, he needs sun.

As naturally we want to include you, please let me know IMMEDIATELY the dates of your spring vacation. I realize you haven't even thought about Christmas yet, but you know I like to plan early. You can find out the dates from the college calendar or whatever. We wouldn't want to write the dean's office to find out a minor thing like that.

I always think of the Varadero trip. Remember how happy we all were at that time?

Your father says if you have forgotten how to write you can always phone. I don't know whether he would accept reversed charges but I would my Johnnycake! I suggest therefore you make it some time during the day.

Snuggles and hugs.
Mummy

John made a paper airplane of the letter, but its first flight was only a halfhearted couple of feet onto the mound of confusion and procrastination on the desk. Abruptly John stood up and wheeled around, as if his mother had entered the room. *He gets so used up.* How completely she gave herself away, even in such a short letter! John crossed his arms over a melancholy ache pouring into his chest; he thought it must have had to do with Ptolemy.

Or with Varadero. The glory of the trip had been having all that time with Grampa Newson. Exuberance! That morning in the Club de Oficiales (it was long before Castro) at Matanzas, waiting to meet the cruise boat with Gramps's friends aboard, whatever-their-names, and Gramps doing that handstand on the dock as the launch came alongside, a salute, a greeting with a septuagenarian's wild flair—his gold watch sliding down out of his vest and hanging safe on its chain; his white suede shoes, caked with whiting which came off on *everything*, hovering in the air in total relaxation; his inverted face, purple with love of life and joy at seeing upside-down friends and delight in showing off.

—— Hey, *Fist!*

John went to the windows, a pair of casements with diamond-shaped lights set in lead sash bars—windows that had once struck him as the perfectly fitting outlook of Higher Education as She Is Diddled at Sheldon Coll.— and he saw, on the path in the courtyard three flights down, Breed with his sleek face turned up, Breed impeccable, sporting a knitted tie, cheerful-looking, crisp, impatient.

John cranked open one of the windows, and Breed called up:

—— How about a bite?

—— O.K. I'll get dressed.

—— Shake a leg. I'll go on over.

—— Emil's?

—— Where else?

—— Order me some scrambled eggs.

3

As John took a stool next to Breed's at the counter, he became vaguely aware of an odor of ozone, a faint suggestion of short circuits, Lionel trains, old sparking electric fans.

Hadn't he noticed the same weak smell the night before? In the car? Was it impacted in his own sinuses? Hell, probably just a toaster here, or a big electric coffee machine, in the chrome tank of one of which John now saw himself attenuated, a dozen feet tall.

Breed looked sharp as always. Not only did he have patches on the elbows of his brand-new jacket; the sleeve ends, also, were piped in neat-stitched cinnamon-colored leather. Crimson vest. That supercock tie. Blond hair

declaratively long—not just let go, for the temples were
trimmed and square-shaven, but a heavy straight combed
mass going back and making an oval bulge of the oc-
ciput: a longhead. Steel-rimmed glasses, steel-ball irises.
Breed just looked bright as hell—but what could you tell
by *appearances*?

—— You look as if you were going to a wedding.

Breed, grinning: —— I made my eight-ten.

John: —— What do you know? I cut a class.

—— Hey, the over-achiever unlaxing!

—— I feel great. (John pounded his chest, then
mock-coughed.)

Breed: —— What got into you?

John felt himself beginning to bristle. Breed's beautiful square teeth; that word, over-achiever. John had
known Chum Breed for only a couple of weeks; he had
glided out of nowhere to become some kind of intimate
—the way, apparently, of sophomore year, when all the
first-year relationships were subject to sharp review and
new shallow enthusiasms drifted in and out. John was not
even sure where he had met Breed—was it having lunch
with a crowd over in the Forrestal Complex, or at a *séré-
nade de merde* in Ackercocke's room? Shadowy man who
wore jackets and neckties to classes, yet along with the
sleekness there was energy, enthusiasm, an air of experience—name it and he had done it: surfing at La Jolla
("Hang ten," he would sometimes cry when an argument
was building like a comber), not bothering to riot at the
second (i.e., best) Newport Festival, pooh-poohing the
black humorists, sniffing airplane glue (at age fourteen),
reading Jorge Luis Borges in Spanish. Not James Baldwin
—LeRoi Jones. Not *Lord of the Flies* (my heavens!)—
Pincher Martin. A hint of something way, way out; yet a
mixer-attender, this dapper cover, this look of totally

14

belonging—to what? Grotesquely inappropriate nickname. Disenchanted way of looking at things, a scoffing
at any act the least bit tainted with college spirit or do-
goodism—he had hooted at the Mississippi volunteers. In
fact, scorn was Breed's basic mode. John had a feeling of
Breed's having fastened on him somehow. . . . The accident the night before was at the back of John's mind, and
Breed's driving so coolly away from it. Yes, the veiled
note of derision, as Breed asked what had got into him, to
cut a class.

—— I decided it was too far to walk.

—— Too far?

—— When I first woke up, I just decided I couldn't
make it, not on foot anyway.

—— Too far to where?

—— Out to Humblesmith.

—— It's not that far out there.

—— It's far when you're going to Hum Sock 23.

—— Oh, Gawd.

—— Overview. Helicopter hop across the Western
tradition. Professor Orreman at the controls.

—— I heard he was pretty good. (Scorn, but a reverse twist when needed.)

—— Oval Ears? Oh, he's good all right.

Emil, the counterman, wearing an appetite-killer of
an apron, slid two thick plates in front of Breed and John
and said: —— How you want your coffee?

Breed said: —— Tea for me.

Emil, a heavy town man, a sincere college-hater,
ducked his head, drew the bowstring of his eyebrows
down to the tip of his nose, and fired a real spitball of a
glance at Breed: —— Cream or lemon? (There was a
lifted-pinkie lilt to the question.)

—— Neither one.

15

John took black coffee and tasted his eggs. Breed, this neat person, seemed to throw his arms around his plate and hug it, and he gobbled.

Breed, his mouth full: —— Why too far to walk?

John put his fork down. Where had all his hunger gone? He said: —— Ever read *Washington Square*? In those days it seems you had this hush downtown there so thick that nobody could *do* anything. Such a great distance between people. Whatshisname, the hero if you could call him that, I forget his name, could barely manage to kiss Catherine Sloper (I remember *her* name. Sloper! Zow! What a name for a feminine lead!)—whatshisname could barely bring himself to kiss her on the cheek. Today, my God, what a different story—so *crowded*. Take the Square itself. I used to go down there some last year, weekends, I was making the coffeehouses and the singing for a while there; it's so crowded you've got nothing but jostling, high-pitched voices, sex right out there in the sun. The kooks are spilling over into the park from the— what do the Hum Sock boys call it?—the inner city? A boggle of women comes running over to the cops screaming: —— Look over there by the railing of the playground, there's a big man exposing himself to the toddlers in the sandboxes. So the cops go over and start walking him away, and then a whole other set of women comes screaming: —— You beasts, what're you doing to that poor man? Brutality! Brutality! Where are you taking him?

—— *This* is why you cut Human Society 23?

—— I feel crowded out there. Oval Ears gives his lectures in that amphitheater in Humblesmith. It's *jammed*.

—— How many?

—— I feel as if the rejects are all there.

—— Rejects?

—— Five apply, one gets in? I feel as if the ones who didn't make it are there, in spirit. All sardined in among the one-armed desks. They have to stand. We're sitting.

Breed really liked this. Those steel ball bearings of his behind the wire-rimmed glasses glistened, and his perfect upper lip curled: —— Wonderful!

—— I feel as if they're all looking at me. How the devil did *I* get to sit there?

—— Don't blame the devil.

—— They make me feel as if I'd shouldered them aside.

—— You've been getting good marks, haven't you?

Marks? What had marks to do with it? Marks were easy. A matter of figuring out what was wanted; catering service. Marks had never been much of a problem. In high school most of the teachers had been women, cinches all. Miss Edith Flan. Mrs. Curbelow. A moment's picture in John's mind: a corridor of Provender Annex, grayish tile walls, glistening rows of lockers, the floor a design of swoops of a rotary waxer; a whispered conference against the baffle of an open locker door with Jeremy Ferne about some skulduggery of Jerry's, but an eye out, a yearning for Madeline to walk past, the desperate, everlasting wish that an indefinite "it" could happen, that she would give a sign, that somehow it would happen to one.

—— Have I told you about my high-school friend Jerry?

—— I don't think so.

—— We spat on the entire works—got on a kick of breaking up organizations, for one thing. Oh, we ruined the P. H. S. Dramatic Society in six weeks flat. Jerry was something—redhead through and through.

But John had already lost interest in telling about Jerry. Had that dirty word, over-achiever, made him want to prove to Breed that he was capable of being *against*? The whole layout at Provender had been pretty standard, and presumably that was what Jeremy Ferne had hated: Parents' meeting every once in a while on a desperate topic like Dating Patterns, really to talk about kids driving across the New York State line in order (as the parents saw it) to you-know-what first, in some cheap tavern, and then you-know-what afterward, right in the family car; that thirteen-year-old taken to Juvenile Court for handing out Seconal capsules, which he'd snitched from the bathroom medicine cabinet at home, to eight of his classmates; the boy named Upshur, son of a vice-president of a decorating-fabric company in the city, hauled up for breaking and entering four separate times—had a morbid weakness for hi-fi gimcracks and doohickies.

But John had been Mr. Reliable, Jr., at least until Jeremy Ferne had come along. Jeremy—born in one of the years when those names were in the wind, Jennifer, Abigail, Deirdre, John spelled Jon; with that name he had to be a no-sayer. What fun they had had! The scenery for *Outward Bound* never got finished; the leading girl quit three days before the performance under the sting of Jerry's direction; on the big night the lighting blew the fuses four times according to plan; Jerry and he took the ticket money and got tight on it. . . .

Breed wiped his mouth and said: —— You know what I think you should do?

—— What's that?

—— I think you ought to walk out to Humblesmith. I mean right now. To see whether it really is too far.

John was aware again of that electrical smell, and he called to the counterman: —— Hey, Emil, you got something shorted in here? Something's frizzing.

Emil shrugged and held the shrug a long time, until he had given John more answer than he had asked for.

John felt irritable. He resented Breed's suggestion. He had a suspicion that Breed was somehow trying to worm into his life.

John said: —— Can we have our check, Emil?

Breed: —— I'd like to come and talk with you some time when that fink Flack isn't around. I've got a proposition I think might interest you.

Breed's eyes glinted with affectionate good humor.

4

HERE the town was thinning out. The flaky slate slabs of the sidewalk, heaved by the frosts of many winters, were tilted and lip-cracked, and John saw chisel marks along the edges of the stone. Yellow and orange leaves were falling through a windless air, and a wonderful luminosity, too, seemed to be drifting down from the maple trees, so that the faces of students who were striding both ways along the sidewalks, holding books against their swinging thighs, murmuring and sometimes laughing, glowed with an unearthly healthiness.

As he walked John fell into a mood of yearning. He saw the deep copper of a spindle tree at the corner of a lawn; his father, who in the years of his disappointment had clung to yard work as if he had a desperate stake in all that was tame in nature, had drummed the names of the domesticated shrubs and trees into John's ears: spindle tree, *Euonymus alatus*, here, with the little wings on the branches and these glorious dark red leaves in the fall. John could not have accounted for the vague familiar desire he had begun to feel now, longing, wanting to find something: a cosmic, all-embracing, doctrinal, permanent something (far beyond red leaves, at which he suddenly felt a little tug of anger) that would be worth working for—worth walking for.

Too far to walk? Was it a matter of objectives? Walking out to Humblesmith in this air that was like ginger ale—there was no lecture waiting for him from Orreman of the Greek Ideal. He had, he remembered, once walked halfway across New Hampshire. That had been a time (three years before?) when he had been irrepressibly eager and earnest. The Presidential Trail. The great thing about that kind of hiking had been that there had never been any particular objective, for the tramping itself was what mattered, the pull of the knapsack shoulder straps, the serene dappled shade along the paths. He remembered now, though, a moment of fury: a knob of Mount Madison, a natural picnic spot with a broad view of green and purple hills, huckleberry bushes close at hand, ironwood, outcroppings of gray lichened rocks—and a litter of Schlitz beer cans on the pathside, Saranwrap blown into sprigs of juniper, an aluminum pan for Sara Lee brownies left beside blackened stones set up to grill Roesseler franks, as the carton lying there testified; the filthy, selfish carelessness of those who thought the American mountains were simply theirs to enjoy and besmear.

With the fanning up of that old out-of-the-way flicker of outrage John found himself now very annoyed with Breed. The idea that he, John, was actually walking out here, as Breed had suggested, to see whether it really was too far, galled him, and so did the thought that Breed liked to watch people; sat with his head tilted and that faint smile on his lips—watching.

John heard himself saying out loud: —— Let's see now.

He looked quickly about—could not perceive that anyone was laughing at a midmorning sidewalk deadhead muttering to himself.

He crossed Seminary Road, and on the right the broad expanse of Planique Fields opened up, the chewed-over gridirons of intramural clubs, at a level somewhat below that of the streetway, with useless, waist-high, paint-peeled wooden fences all around and two rows of goal posts standing like so many reproachful fresh-air-mad Christers on parade. Beyond there was a slum of lush swamp trees festooned with murderous honeysuckle. Humblesmith, the stadium, and the new gray buildings of the Institute were ahead, after these fields.

He felt that he was on the edge of a dangerous state of mind. Breed had stung him. A reckoning? should he make a reckoning? All right, to begin with, he who yearned to be different wore a Sheldon College uniform—corduroys, plaid shirt with button-down collar, pullover sweater, more-or-less white sweat socks, one loafer sole bound, around and around, with dirty adhesive tape; a look of caring about not caring about appearances, which were, on principle, deceptive anyway. Underneath—he took showers. He was thin; he knew that the strain of the Sheldon overload showed in the rigidity of his neck muscles. Although inwardly not exactly dynamic, he tried at least to be equable most of the time, kept up a steady cheerful front, which was more than a lot of these self-consciously surly types did. He could talk—in a rhythm of pauses and little explosions—but he felt he was shy

22

and reserved (like his father?), and perhaps because of
this diffidence Flack, on two beers, once, had called him
supercilious, a superior bastard. But Flack was a retarded
child, everyone knew that. One problem John felt he did
have: an evasive eye. He sometimes found himself, offset-
ting this, gazing deeply into the eye of the person with
whom he was talking.

Too far to walk? What had happened to the zest he
had had during those years in Provender Annex? Third in
his class—only Jerry and a girl ahead of him; president of
the Senate; editor of *Falling Leaves;* tennis team. *Nex!
Nex! Rah Rah Provender!* What a shock to land in a whole
bog of class presidents and valedictorians at Sheldon. His
father, himself once a class president, but once more than
just that, too: sensitive, bursting with ideas—and now,
$38,000 per annum, wheeler-dealer in a big reproduction-
of-colonial-furniture company in Worcester, Massachu-
setts; disappointed, disappointing man. His mother—
she'd given up teaching in the dim past to apply her firm
attention to the brood; she *called* it the brood. They lived
in a house with a glass wall staring into the teeth of a
house without a glass wall across the street. . . .

Oooh, the way Breed had driven away from that
sound of screeching tires. How did one deal with that? By
saying "Brother"? . . .

How did one deal with Sheldon College?

What a struggle it had been to get in! And then: He
had been on the Dean's list as a freshman, but progres-
sively through the first term he had felt let down and in
the second simply bored. During his last year at Provender he had at least had a couple of really exciting courses
—a Shakespeare seminar of only six kids, and Mrs. Curbelow's acid and lucid bit on the patterns of American
mentality. But as a freshman at Sheldon he had caught

three graduate students as instructors, all dull typicals, one fairly good full-fledged but brand-new Ph.D., and one full professor, a dodo with copper-coated arteries, a (barely) living reproach to the theory of tenure who had obviously been sloughed off onto freshman duty-courses by his sharper departmental colleagues. The assignments of freshman year had been either indigestible gobbets of rote learning which the instructors distastefully regarded as remedial, or monstrous chores of reading—for every Sheldon teacher seemed to believe that the paperback revolution had been achieved precisely in order to enable *his* students to read everything ever written about *his* discipline. Five to seven endless tomes a not-endless week. If it was Publish or Perish for the profs, it was, for the students who encountered the fruits of that policy, a choice of Skip or Flip.

But this year all that had faded into something completely different and very hard to put a finger on: a kind of life-fuzziness, a feeling of being immured from the bright outdoor light of reality. John now had begun to wonder why he was at Sheldon at all, for he wasn't getting one tenth out of the place, or putting one hundredth into it, of what he should be. Above all, he felt like a popgun that wasn't being aimed. Any minute there might be a pointless muffled bang, aimed at nothing, at absolute random, and the cork would fly to the end of the string. Why? What the hell was he doing here?

Here? John found himself standing on the granite steps of Humblesmith. How far had it been, walking out here? Students were entering and leaving, and the brass latch bar of the door rattled again and again. The building was heavy, dark, fortified, Norman. John turned, to start back, all the pleasure of cutting the class drained away. He felt his arm gripped by strong fingers.

The rostrum voice: —— Walk along with me a bit.

—— Oh, good morning, sir.

Orreman. A drift of silver-white hair, which always looked newly shampooed; goldfish-bowl glasses, undoubtedly post-cataract; the famous ears of the nickname, thick wrinkled parabolic slabs of purple next to the white. The grip eased from a cop's move-along-buddy hold into a pseudo-parental caress, and the old man's hand stayed embarrassingly there. From the end of the off arm dangled an ancient brown leather briefcase held together by straps of frayed webbing.

Orreman: —— Enjoy that this morning? I love that lecture!

John: —— Yeah, that was great, sir.

Yes, Oval Ears loved his old nuggets. (*Take these down, take 'em down and memorize 'em and live by 'em —the Seven Wise Men. Cleobulus of Rhodes: Moderation is the chief good. Periander of Corinth: Forethought in all things. Pittacus of Mytilene: Know thine opportunity. Bias of Priene: Too many workers spoil the work. Thales of Miletus: If you go on a man's bond, ruin is near. Chilo of Sparta: Know thyself. Solon of Athens: Nothing in excess.*) His love of these old, old lectures, which he must have pieced together long before Scotch Tape was invented, really his self-love—this was what made him so good: integrity, seeing *nothing* through those thick lenses, absolutely no fear of death. It was thrilling to listen to such a hero—the timbre, not the substance. Right now as they walked he was kneading John's arm, feeling out the rubbery fullness of a youth's muscles. The old philosopher's pace, intended to be springy, was a kind of rhythmic lurch, for Orreman rose far up on his toes with each step, giving himself good reason to hang on to a student.

25

John thought it was curious that he had not admitted cutting the lecture.

—— The point is: the ram, the he-goat, the dove, fishes, sparrows, the hare, the swan, the dolphin . . . Aphrodite's creatures. . . . Add the idea of the goat's singing voice—

The point was that there was no point. It was the passion of the old man, the mysterious tremor in the voice, the conceit, that attracted even the most disenchanted and cynical students—and it was precisely those things John had decided to *cut*. He wanted to shake off the old hand on his arm. He only wanted to hear from the brilliant young innovators who sliced across the modern disciplines with no somatic vibrations at all: Cranston, Aronstein, Gutwillig; who were shaping *new* configurations for *this* world. John and the professor walked along in silence, there being nothing further to say. They passed the noble bronze spindle tree.

Orreman: —— What was the name again, young man?

—— Fist, sir. John Fist.

The old man turned his eyes, immensely magnified by the glasses, on John, and they were milked over now with something like cataracts of thought. John saw perspiration on the veined upper lip. Was it *painful* for Orreman to put on this jig-jog show of vigor?

—— Ah. Yes. I have a paper of yours.

He stopped, let go of John's arm, and began to tug at the belts of webbing on his briefcase. The teeth of the buckles would not readily give up the frayed fabric, and the old man jerked so hard a couple of times that grunts were wrenched from his chest, if not the straps from their fastenings.

—— Oversight. *Hurrunch!* Wretched thing. Thought

I'd handed out all these papers this morning. Found yours after class.

Again John failed to mention his absence.

The old man, finally getting the briefcase open, raised one knee on which to table it as he fished for the paper and drew it out from the chaos within, at which John felt he should not look, as if it were an old man's long winter underwear showing. Orreman held the paper up close to his eyes, and he cleared his throat.

—— Oh yes yes yes. I am sorry to say I've given you a D.

John felt a bolt of anger; he would have liked to turn on his heel and walk away as the old man grabbled again at the straps. But before he knew it, the cop grip, followed by the loving squeeze, was on his biceps again, and they were bouncing along again, and now something extraordinary began. The old man had apparently corrected the paper himself (among how many others?), and though he could not recall John's name, he remembered every sentence of the essay.

It is now August of the year 441. I was chosen to present a tetralogy at Dionysia this year partly because my uncle happens to be a close friend of the archon eponymus, *who selects the poets. . . .*

—— The device is clever. (John really felt now that he was a Seeing Eye dog leading a blind man along the street; yet he was an unreliable guide who might dump the ancient toe dancer in a ditch or an open manhole, if they came to one—now trembling with hurt, dismay, and anger over that D, for he remembered with particular pain his spurning of Breed's toothsome question:

—— You've been getting good marks, haven't you?) And I liked the temple scene in your first tragedy, as you describe it. (*The rocky island of Aegina, in the*

*Saronic Gulf, has suffered a plague sent by Hera, wildly
jealous because the name of the place memorializes one
of her husband Zeus's sexual conquests. Aeacus, the king,
going to the temple of Zeus to plead for relief, comes on
an oak tree whose trunk crawls with an enormous swarm
of ants. In the temple he cries out to be given a man for
every ant. . . .*) But then you try to use the Myrmidons, the
ant men, in some sort of up-to-date sociological way, Fist.
It's shallow. Not true to your promising departure.
Shallow. Besides, you've picked a year in which it's folly
to compete: You're up against the *Antigone*.

The old man fell quiet. He seemed to be breathing
through a wire screen in his windpipe. The professorial
hand slid around John's upper arm and hugged it to the
tweedy professorial shoulder. Had he sensed John's
anger, and was he forgiving John for it?

—— Fist, I had your father twenty-six years ago.

John realized that *that* was what had been crowding
into those huge eyes when Orreman had first looked
around at him at the sound of the name. Fist! Fist!

—— God, sir, don't I know it? He's told me (a careful
tone of horror) seven hundred times.

—— Is that why you picked me? (But John had no
time furiously to deny it, for the voice, quavering a little
now, went straight on.) He seemed very tall and slender.
Wore bow ties, I remember. He was involved somehow in
a nasty struggle for control of Alpha Delt—I never knew
exactly what part he played in it. But I liked him, anyway. He had a very nice poetic-argumentative side. . . .
What has he ever done with himself?

John was staggered for a moment by the thought
that Mr. Orreman—suddenly he was Mister—had bottled
and corked his father, aged twenty, and preserved him all
these years exactly as he had been back then. Very tall

and slender. And so he still was today, minor pot excepted. But poetic-argumentative? The generation before his father's had been overpowering—the professor was a senile remnant of it, John supposed. His father's father had been a *strict* man, and Malcolm Fist seemed to shrink, purse up, when he told stories of Grandfather Fist roaring Latin declensions at the head of the dinner table. Nowadays John's father was a stiff, kindly man, exhibiting a stone Palladian façade (had the classical ornamentation come partly from this gripping, bouncing vitality alongside John?) behind which one could, with persistence, find a shy, warm, lonely human figure. Why couldn't he just relax and show his feelings? Was he afraid of being hurt? By a son? John often had the feeling that his father was baffled by him, and even a little afraid of him. The downhill career—as John saw it—might have had something to do with this remoteness; or vice versa. Apprenticeship with Hakkainen, the brilliant designs for modern lamps in his own name, the tie-in with Illumicon, then those queer years of half business, half critic-and-teacher, then poof, Colonial Crafts, Inc. One couldn't say he'd been pushed—by his wife, by "the brood." He had chosen. Sold out attic to cellar. Against the current of his anger John angrily thought: If only he had been a sonofabitching brute!

John answered, cool: —— He's in the fake antique furniture business. Very successful.

—— What a pity. (No emphasis.)

For a crazy moment John thought he was on the edge of tears. He was very much drawn to Mr. Orreman, and very much afraid of him.

5

JOHN, trying to study, sat facing his desk and steadfastly
kept his back to Wagner, who had clumped in and top-
pled like a falling monster into Flack's easy chair and was
periodically clearing his throat to give notice that conversation would be welcome—ahem, any time, kha-kha-
kha-hem, no hurry.

John outlasted him, and Wagner finally said:

—— Fist, what the hell are those numbers up there?

John gave up, wheeled around, and said: —— Magic
square. Haven't you ever seen a magic square?

Against the wall above the chaos of his desk, perhaps
to propitiate the forces of derangement in his life, John
had tacked a rectangle of corrugated cardboard from a

carton, on which, with a Magic Marker, he had inscribed a magic square:

8	1	6
3	5	7
4	9	2

—— Any way that you add a row—up, down, across, diagonally—it comes out the same.

—— My God! Fifteen. Fifteen! My God. That's really marvelous.

Wagner was wearing a tie and jacket—evidently fully ready to go to the dining hall and eat, though it was only half past four.

It was always a mistake for Wagner to button his shirt collar and put on a tie. This backed blood up into his head and besides giving a sidewise-slanting set of bulges to his forehead, of puffed veins, making him look as if he would tip over, also seemed to start, possibly by a flushing out of his brain, some process in mimicry of deep thought. When his skull was thus blood-logged, Wagner would work up to a burst of Wagner-wisdom or Wagner-wit at the end of a sentence and then with great quickness add, "The . . . um . . . ," as if he had meant to go right on into a triumphant new sentence but felt on second thought that he should give a decent pause for agreement, admiring laughter, or at least reflection.

Wagner was made of splendid meat. Indeed he was well on his way, as a mere sophomore, to a realization of his whole life's ambition—the right to buy a sweater with an "S" on it; he was a third-string guard on the football team. On the defense. He had a bruise on his right cheek from Wednesday's scrimmage.

For reasons John had not been able to puzzle out, Wagner thought the world of him. Wagner's admiration was touching, but it was also a source of chagrin, partly because John had long since ceased to admire himself, so that Wagner's hero worship of him seemed not only misplaced but gratuitous. On objective evidence, besides, Wagner, though already a campus success, appeared to be a big fool, and this did not throw a pleasing light on his choice of John for high regard. John had the consolation, though in truth a weak one, that Wagner admired a large number of people. Wagner's greatest fault was being Generous. His next greatest fault was being Very Enthusiastic.

Still checking the rows of the magic square:

—— God, Fist, where did you ever dig that up? That's really super.

To get into Sheldon, Wagner must have achieved S.A.T. scores well up in the six hundreds, perhaps in the seven hundreds; he was undoubtedly bright—but this fact did not of course prevent him from also being stupid.

Wagner: —— Say, what're you doing about your major? Deadline's Tuesday, you know, that prelim option thing.

—— I haven't decided. That blank doesn't mean anything, does it?

—— I figure English. I mean I'm going to do law, and my father says the law schools all complain about their students can't put together a decent sentence. The . . . um . . .

In the ringing pause John experienced an uncomfortable sensation—could it have been a twinge of covert envy of Wagner? This man went in straight lines, never vacillated. Surely that unpleasant throb was a wish that he, John, could be so full of purpose, so set, so doubtless, lower jaw pushed out, just so, as the ice-breaking ship offers the floe its forefoot. John thought: I mustn't let his liking me make me like him.

John: —— My trouble is, I want to major in everything. I want to be like that Gutwillig character, slice right through all the listings in the lousy catalogue. Boy, what a polyhistor that cat is!

Wagner's eyes were getting big, and the glow of his wonder at John was suffusing his face, lending the bruise a fresh lividity. John could see that Wagner wanted to ask what a polyhistor was but also wanted to pretend he knew, and John wondered whether he had used the word in order to produce just such a silly tension in Wagner.

Wagner: —— I thought you were thinking of getting with Orreman. I heard you say a couple of weeks ago—

John: —— *Orreman!* Where'd you get *that* idea? He's shallow. He's really shallow.

Yes, that was the word the old man had used about *him.* In two days the shock of the D had by no means abated. John felt that all his work at Sheldon was worthless, worthless. You couldn't sell that essay, or anything he'd ever written, on a street corner for the price of a single copy of *Mad.* You couldn't trade "My Tetralogy" for an apple. What was the use of this stupid grind, in which a single letter, an "A," or a "D," or even an "S," meant both nothing and so much?

Devoted. Demented. Drunk. Distinguished. Daring. Dignified. Donne. Dante. Dostoevski. Daydream. Diaphragm. Detumescence.

Dumbbell. D was for dumbbell. D would forever be for Dumbbell.

Wagner: —— Heck, you wouldn't want to get into that Gutwillig crowd, would you? That creep Spinter?

—— Who he?

33

—— Haven't you heard about him? He's the creep that's organizing the Student Freedom Union or whatever he calls it, something like that.

—— What's *that*? Sounds awful.

—— Where have you been? I'm surprised at you, Fist. You're a Gutwillig boy and don't know about all that cruddy bunch? Those dormitory Maoists? The . . . um . . .

John reflected that Wagner's father would undoubtedly use the same words in the same cadences and the same tone. John didn't know Wagner's father, but Wagner was the sort of guy who would have the sort of father whom Wagner would sound just like. You could hear the resonance of genes in the son.

—— Never heard of them. I don't follow all those campus rumblings much. Anyway, I'm no Gutwillig boy, as you put it. I only said . . .

But John broke off. He was thinking of Sidney Gutwillig's coldness, the way the young professor seemed to calculate every utterance for effect, his detachment, his cleverness—his essential iciness. He was brilliant, though: he really did know everything. And all of the everything he knew he turned, with a knife-edge rational plausibility, to (as he would be apt to say) analysis of the humanity-locus—meaning, presumably, wondering where the hell we are now. The trouble was his frigid, inhuman, cerebral detachment; Maoists and Y.A.F.s and civil-rights activists and student-senate Birchites and Du Bois Clubbers were all the same to him, as long as they were against the Establishment. Gutwillig had no hot coals in him—no magic.

—— I want to major in magic. I want to be a magician. A physicist-architect. A psychiatrist-ecologist. A geneticist-politician. I want to be able to use calculating machines from A to Z, you know, devise the dog tag with all your medical and emotional and educational history

34

on it, everything about you, which you wear around your neck at all times, and then, you see, when you have to make a decision you just insert the dog tag into a Fist Machine, a thing like a vending machine, along with a data ticket with your question on it and *whirrr!*

—— Boy, you're sick. (Said with a look of *great* admiration.)

A feeling of exultation was swelling in John as he thought and talked further to this uncritical devotee about becoming someone who might, one day, help control the forces of nature without resorting to prayer or hymn singing or psalm reading or genuflection (he saw his mother dipping a knee in the aisle) or wafer eating or even—belief. There was a vastness in his discontent that seemed to give him an actual physical chill. The most outstanding men were so unutterably puny—sharp Gut-willig, noble Orreman, Cranston, Aronstein, his father and his father's father, and good God (Who is not-God), what about Breed, Wagner, Ackercocke, Flack, Gibbon, Fist? Ants, tiny crawlers in a swarm on a dead tree trunk. John wanted, now with a soaring elation, to work on the machine that would unlock the riddle of Everything. There must be answers, better answers. *There must be a way.*

Wagner, being swept along on the flood of John's excitement, which was now incredibly vague, grandiose, and thrilling, began to want reassurance: —— Don't shit me, Fist.

—— Oh, come on, Wagner, loosen up.

An exuberant laugh broke from John's mouth. Choose a major? He'd *never* choose a major field.

—— You sound like Chum Breed. (Pain in this utterance, because Breed was evidently not among those whom Wagner admired.)

—— *He* gets the idea of my machine. (But John had

never discussed it with Breed, having just thought it up.)

—— Now you're really going through your hat. I'm getting off that guy. He toys with people—know what I mean? He drags a guy down.

While still riding his euphoric cloud, John began to feel a sensation of having the brakes on; a squirt of retro rockets. Abruptly he changed his tone: —— You know how Gibbon talks about the negos and the posos—positive and negative guys? Breed's your real prime nego. But if you ask me, it's all a front, it's a mask he wears. I think it's just a cover-up—for some kind of weakness. He denies everything because he repudiates himself—right? I had a friend in school like that.

Wagner: —— You're scared of him. Just like me.

—— Breed? Don't be funny.

—— He's the one behind Siddle quitting. You know that?

—— What do you mean, quitting?

—— Siddle resigned. He's gone home. The other day, Thursday I think it was.

—— Oh, baby! These big identity-crisis types who run off and get a job picking Brussels sprouts in the Imperial Valley and come back the next year with a brand-new personality as the new Albert Camus.

—— Breed did it to him. He really screwed him up for fair.

—— Look. (As if to say: —— Breed can't touch me.) I've already done my dropping out: I was a dropout from my mother's lap.

—— Har-de-har.

John was dissatisfied with the outcome of Wagner's having barged in. He now felt the way he most particularly hated to feel: cautious. Maybe he'd better think about that option slip on the majoring business.

6

On the next Thursday night, late, Fist was working in his
room by himself, and within the clear-cut cone of yellow-
white that hung from a Tensor lamp lay a library book he
was reading, Köhler's *The Mentality of Apes,* inert on his
knee. He had just broken its spine by bending its cover-
boards back on each other—something his father had told
him, many years before, *never* to do; said it was as wrong
as killing an animal. John had done it this time to shock
himself, to clear his eyes. By this hour heavy-headed and
played out, he had a sensation of having been groping
without aim or need across a simply boundless evening.

—— Flack around?

John jumped. He hadn't heard the door open. At
first, just having lifted his eyes from the light-bathed

37

page, he could make out nothing in the dim room. Then he saw a glistening row of teeth floating in mid-air, and he knew they were Breed's excellent set. Breed's smile of ingratiation.

—— Oh it's you. (Rather listless greeting.) No, he went to the movies. *Marriage Italian Style*. You see it?

The teeth floated closer, ever smiling: pleased that the famous fink was not home. Breed was smoking; smoke was coming out between the teeth.

—— No, I haven't. They say it's sort of nyaa.

—— I don't know (lukewarm even in truculence; a feeling of a fog in the room), Ackercocke said Loren was great—twice as big as life was what he said.

—— What time did he go?

—— Flack? Late show I guess.

—— Then we can talk.

For a moment John wished Flack hadn't gone out—or wished, at least, that he could defend Flack to Breed; for if he couldn't manage even a minimal loyalty to the man with whom he had decided to room of his own volition, then he must be proven, in Breed's eyes, a poor picker, or a sucker. With a mild stirring of resentment John told himself (but not Breed) that Chum made too much of a thing of Flack's being, as he put it, an Untouchable.

—— Ever see the knight's-move magic square?

Now above the teeth John could see the brilliant black of Breed's eyes, coming forward and changing into onyxes in the layered reflections of the tiny lamp, staring at the design of numbers over the desk.

—— I think I may be able to remember it. Got something I can write on?

John handed Breed a pad and a pen. Breed pushed aside papers and the *Apes* in the pool of light and bent over, swiftly hatching lines.

BOOK ONE

He said as his hand flew: —— I used to dabble in all
this crap—ever fool with ciphers? Look. Here's the idea.
(Was something hot? The Tensor lamp?) You have a
chessboard, eight rows of squares, see? Now starting from
his position between the bishop and the rook, that's the
number one, the knight tours the board, never touching
the same square twice. (Breed's hand was jumping
swiftly, following the path of the knight's crooked moves,
jotting in a number for each stop, two, three . . . ten,
eleven . . . amazing speed: thirty-two, thirty-three . . .),
until . . . (He paused, chewed his lip, went on:) There!
Now add! Every row across or down gives two hundred
and sixty.

John, poring over the diagram, thinking of himself as
an awful Wagner once removed: —— Incredible. That's
really something.

What was hard to believe was not the thing itself but
rather Breed's fluidity, his pulling that complex memory
of sixty-four numbered spaces right out of the smoke that
wreathed his head. John had for a moment a strong feeling of Jerry Ferne back at Provender—of being dared
somehow to let go. Breed had pulled back into the shadows, moving like a night animal.

—— How the devil do you remember all that?

Breed laughed, with an outblowing, hissing sound,
and said: —— I can visualize the course of the tour. It
gets sticky around the low forties. . . . But I'm surprised
at you, John, if you're interested in these things. . . .

Breed left the challenge hanging. John looked at the
chessboard and numbers again, to see if he could find
whatever it was that Breed meant, but in his gaze the
figures blurred. John's hands felt cold; he was still hearing that hiss.

—— The diagonals don't check out. Each one is four
off.

39

Breed went on to say something about no one's ever having achieved a perfect knight's-move magic square, and the difficulties . . . but John was remembering Breed-isms from other times and talks. *The minute you make a commitment to another person you find you're committed to disappointment.* . . . *"Rah"—the last outcry of mediocrity.* . . . *Life here is one interminable TV commercial.* . . . The prime nego. How he ridiculed Wagner's resoluteness, Flack's confidence and optimism and little egg crate of squash balls! The catalogues of scorn! Brotherhood Week, *McCall's* on adoption, the moon shots, Martin Luther King's doctrine of love, success, the martyr J.F.K., cars called Dart and Fury with tigertails hanging out of gas tanks, "truth" and Oppenheimer and Teller, together-ness, "doing things," the Community Chest (Jayne Mansfield), L.B.J.'s little leaden-soldier war on poverty: the lists of his disgust had no end.

To John it seemed that the light in the room, or in his own eyes, was growing dimmer: opacity, thickness, diffusion. Again he saw smoke coming out from between clenched teeth.

What was the strange attractiveness of Breed's nihilism? John had always thought of himself as a good boy. He remembered a scene he had thrown when he was about twelve—bedtime, both his parents looking worried beside his bed, he blubbering: he was "different," the guys called him names, Mum and Dad were too strict about not letting him out nights—they were going to turn him into a sissy. How *that* worried each of them for different reasons! He had been too good; he had been a yes-please boy. Breed was all no. Breed had made an entire ideology out of that one negative syllable. John had no such unitary scheme of life: his yes didn't really matter, for his closest approach to a philosophical system lay in mere notions of fairness and unfairness, just not want-ing to be pushed around; somewhere at the fringes was a rather weak belief in loyalty to a few friends. There was his passive political system: be fair (to Fist), don't welsh (on Fist). Beyond this, life was a sleepwalk. He supposed that he was supposed to get a degree. He wandered with glazed eyes and outstretched hands through thickets of college rules, parental permissions, friends' codes, federal and state and local laws, money problems, inner timidi-ties, the pressure of time so strong at table and toilet, the contradiction of drive-a-sharp-deal and give-a-little, as-signments, postponements, papers, tests, a boring system to beat with gimmicks and shortcuts. The enormous reaches of his yearning measured the abyss of uncertainty on the edge of which he walked in this everlasting drow-siness. Breed with his total nego outlook at least seemed wide awake, fully alive; this may have been the pull.

—— How did it turn out the other day? Was it too far to walk out to Humblesmith?

—— I did walk out there (a sheepish smile in the half light), you bastard.

—— I know.

—— How did you know that? (A flash of anxiety, modulating swiftly into annoyance.)

—— My spies.

—— I'm through with Orreman. I've quit going to his class.

Now John really did smell the electrical-burning odor: Was it a factor of his own irritation? Always around Breed. Again the curls of gray smoke coming out from the interstices of Breed's shining grinders; further deepening of John's sense of twilight—his feeling of giving in to what lay behind those glistening teeth. Into utter still-ness, into the heart of the silence that hung so thickly in the room that the smoke seemed, after some moments, unable to move any more, Breed asked:

—— What do you want?

John felt an outpouring of relief. Yes, he *would* try to express what he wanted. So much, so much! It began, surely, with sentience. He wanted to *feel*, to push his personal feelings out to the limits of the galaxies, and inward to the molten pit of the center of the earth. Awareness of the entire works was what he wanted, and to encompass and understand it all! . . . No, now; slow down. . . . The thing was to build up a store of experiences, of events of the senses of every kind and sort, of every possible degree of importance—soak them in, drink them all in, so that one could really get in touch with the solid hardpan reality that must lie underneath all the crap, the dirt, the billboards, the shrubbery. But it wasn't just a matter of going through motions—he wanted to experience a breakthrough, a whole series of real breakthroughs, so marked that you'd inwardly hear each time some sort of loud crack, sonic boom. These would be only instant-long, instants when everything would fall away and naked perception and feeling, truth, the pure only thing, would be right there: all the walls would come tumbling down that most of the time shut John away from other human beings, from trees, from sea water, from light, from air to breathe. These moments would be somehow mystical, because the distinction between John Fist and the tree, the crag, the girl's hand, the shell on the beach, would disappear entirely, and John and the object would be inextricably intermixed as one significant fused piece of the answer. The ineffable would in those moments come clear. The meaning of everything would be right there in some minuscule detail, some minor whorl of the shell—exactly corresponding with a little whorl in John's thumbprint. The whole thing would probably be right outside language. And above all, above all: to have this with some person, with a girl. Fusion, a feeling of such closeness that one person would *become* the other. Genuine feeling, openness, impulses right out in the open—until you'd share with another human being a perfect moment of really complete acceptance and understanding, with no part of the self held back, till giving and taking would become a single motionless force: a full stop of simply being.

—— I'll give it all to you. Every bit of it.

Breed had said that. John was not even sure, in the murk of the room and of his mind, that he had spoken aloud about these enormous wants of his. Had Breed *sensed* what he had been thinking?

—— How's that again?

—— I said, I'll give all of it to you. Exactly what you want.

John felt he had to stand up, but he was quite unable to lift himself out of his chair. For a moment he thought his best chance of breaking out of this absurd lock would be to laugh loud and hard: Breed was really pulling his leg for a fare-thee-well. But all that came out was an odd choking sound, devoid of mirth or even of skepticism. John tried nevertheless to carry through the purpose of his half laugh.

—— Hey, the humor around here.

—— I'm perfectly serious. (There was a sternness in these words that gave John a chill; he felt goose pimples spread on his back.) It's all yours.

Now John, beginning to be ashamed of his own adrenals, was able to muster some sincere ridicule: —— How much? (Mildly said, the sarcasm gaining force from understatement in tone of voice.) What's the fee?

—— You're asking for a lot. And so will I.

—— Brother! (That word from the accident on the throughway, that word of inaction, of protest that was really acquiescence.) When you try to put a guy on, you really spread it thick and smelly.

Breed answered by not answering. The silence in the room seemed to develop the pressure of several atmospheres, as if Breed and he were in a soundless cavern deep under green, green water. John had finally to come up for air, and with a splash he broke the silence:

—— What are you saying to me, anyway?

—— I'll put it in plain English: My organization wants to make a deal with you. I'll give you all that you want. You'll pay for this service by turning your id over to me.

—— What do you mean? What are you trying to do —psych me?

—— I want your inmost primeval soul. You can have anything you want for it.

—— Jesus Christ, Breed!

—— Invocations of that kind don't cut any ice with me.

Again Breed let a long silence hang in the room. John wished intensely for Flack—his sky-blue Montana decency; he would switch on the overhead light as he came in the room, and everything would take on hard, familiar outlines. John fell back on something like abuse:

—— You're such a creep, Breed. (Then, too loud:) I'm tired. I've got a lot of work to do. What kind of hell are you trying to put me through?

John could see those teeth, in what must surely have been an indulgent smile; then Breed said: —— Those ideas—of putting somebody "through" hell—are old-fash-

44

ioned, John. As a matter of fact, you might say our organization began to feel crowded in its former premises
(John dimly saw Breed's right forefinger pointing downward, as if toward the boiler rooms of the Painter Complex), and we reluctantly moved up here. It really
shouldn't be any news that Hell is up here now. Perhaps
this is the way to put it: My boss doesn't worry about
Heaven any more—doesn't think of God as his foremost
enemy, or maybe I should say ally, any more. In the
course of the last century, century and a half, the ability
of churches to do evil on earth has fallen off sharply. We
thank the scientists and their pals the manufacturers for
this. Because of all their hardware, daily living has become so much worse that people really need to believe
that things are getting better, and preachers and priests
can't kid them into believing any such thing—only the
politicians and the nationalists can do that. So church
collections have been on the decline, the peasants aren't
turning in their gold earrings any more. The less money
the churches take in, the less influence and power they
dispense, and so much the less they can do *our* work for
us. The Boss's main enemy—I mean, ally—now that the
churches can't help him, is the rational square, the lib-
eral, the city-planner, your anti-poverty warrior, your
decent man, Adlai, the horizontal transcendentalist, the
man who only takes a couple of drinks before dinner,
your brilliant teacher like Gutwillig who after all is a
dull, good, dogged improver in intellectual disguise. You.
You, John Fist.

Now the short-circuit smell was overpowering. John
felt that he was near the center of an enormous electrical
field of force in which something had gone eerily, irre-
parably wrong. Was Breed himself some kind of flesh-

and-blood electronic calculator, his transistors all asmoke, the smoke oozing out through the crevices between his insulator-like teeth?

All John could do was to put out a little explosion of disbelief: —— Organization!

Breed: —— Oh, yes. A very old and sound one. We've had plenty of experience—with better men than you, son. We've made deals with Scaliger, Socrates, Apuleius, Cagliostro. We taught Roger Bacon a thing or two —Very Old Math, I guess you'd have called it. Theophilus of Adana—the Virgin Mary got *him* off. Who do you think lived in the black dog that always trotted beside Cornelius Agrippa of Nettesheim? And how do you think Albertus Magnus was able to conjure up a rose garden for the Emperor from out of the snow, in the dead of winter? . . . Wagner tells me you have some idea of being a necromancer.

John spoke in a kind of groan: —— Who *are* you?

—— You already are a magician (Breed went on, ignoring the question), in the sense that you're a neurotic. Any doc could tell you that you're constantly using a kind of magic in an unconscious attempt to adjust what you experience as the lousy present to what you think of as the lovely past. That's a fine magic—but hopeless. You can do better than that!

—— Who are you? (The groan was louder and sounded this time almost like a threat.)

—— I'm the Spirit of Playing It Cool.

John's incredulity now took a bizarre form: How, he thought, *could* the devil's helper be a sophomore? How could he be someone who drove a car registered in the name of some senior?

—— Names don't matter. Call me Chum. Some of my fellow executives have names you may know. Moloch,

46

Ashtoreth, Belial; Auld Hornie, Puki, Shitface, Tchort, and Pug; Leviathan of Pride, Isacaaron of Lust, Balaam of Buffoonery, Behemoth of Blasphemy. We have a long proud record.

—— How can you give me what I want?

—— You've told me what you want as best you could. The organization is all too familiar with the set of desires you describe: that set has become rather boring to us, to tell the truth. (In the organization we do use this term, sets—new math of the psyche, you might say. Set is the name of a devil in Egypt—there's an irony!) Yours is what we call the Soph Set. *You're ripe for a disastrous slide, Fist.*

—— Leave me alone!

—— In many cases, this past year or two, this particular set has been more aggressive and affirmative in tone than your case is. The desire for fusion et cetera et cetera is all there, but we've been running into a great deal of urge to demonstrate, actually carry signs and sit down in outer offices—in order to get the chancellor bounced, change parietal hours to allow more intercourse in the dorms, all that. Spinter's type of thing, you know about him; that bunch on Gutwillig's coattails. You seem a bit more on the sidelines—so far. Actually, we *like* your kind of detachment, at this stage.

For one wildly happy moment John recaptured the idea that Breed was kidding the hide off him—then that was lost, utterly lost. As the loss hit him John had a kind of double vision—watched himself watching Breed, looked at himself being hypnotized by Breed's black-spark, steel-ball eyes.

—— How long can I have my wishes before you take my—my *soul*, did you say?

—— It doesn't work that way. It used to. When we

47

were downstairs, we used to give a candidate a fixed time,
say twenty-six years, to enjoy things here, and then we'd
snatch him. We haven't that kind of time any more. So
nowadays the deal works concurrently.

—— How do you mean?

—— I mean just that. I give you what you say you
want, and you pay, concurrently. Both things go on at
once. I'm your servant, and you're ours, simultaneously.
The contract runs for twenty-six weeks, and if at the end
of that time both parties are satisfied, we can give you a
lifetime renewal.

—— But just what do you mean by taking my soul?
What do you want of me?

—— We want you to do our work with all your
soul.

—— Your work? What's that?

Breed patted John on the shoulder, and his lips drew
back briefly over his teeth, which opened and closed, so
that the smile seemed like a hungry bite into something
soft.

—— Never mind the details. You'll know when the
time comes. Just do what comes natural. You'll catch
on.

—— And you mean I get what I want at the same
time?

—— Yes! Yes! You can have it both ways! I'll give
you the magic you want! I'll teach you the whole Kab-
balah, the Book of Enoch. I'll show you everything Pope
Sylvester II knew—Michael Scot, Klingsor, Katterfelto,
all the blackest of the black. *Mana, wakan, hasina.*
Philters, scarabs, triskelions, merrythoughts. I'll show you
spells, I'll let you in on rites—how to put yourself in a
state of influence. Live it up, Fist! Wear the Tarnkappe!
Help yourself to those breakthroughs. This is the way to

48

be *alive*. I'm offering you life. Don't go on being one of the walking dead.

John (falling into utter confusion): —— Do I have to grow a beard?

Chum Breed's deep laughter rang through the room like Leporello's *mille e tre!* The laughter rapidly buoyed John's feelings. He, too, felt laughter rising up his windpipe like a series of big bubbles, and then bursting out. He floated up easily out of his chair and felt himself shaking hands with Breed.

—— A little matter of a signature.

Breed had drawn from his pocket a paper covered on both sides with print so fine that John could not possibly have read it, even right under the Tensor lamp, without a magnifying glass. But John was feeling reckless, loose-muscled, free!—and he had not the slightest interest in reading what the paper said. Breed was offering him a ball-point. John spread the paper against the wall and signed in a dim half light. Breed, saying there was also a little matter of a seal, drew out from an inner pocket a small test tube with a swab of cotton and a medical dart in it of the sort doctors use for drawing blood for a smear on a slide. Deftly he cleaned the end of John's right thumb with the cotton—the chill of the alcohol made John shiver to his shoes—and he plunged the dart home so fast John scarcely felt it. At Breed's command John pressed a blob of blood onto the paper beside his signature. Then he fell to his knees and cried out, with a powerful wrench of feeling that was both despair and exultation:

—— Evil, be thou my Good!

7

JOHN saw her first, from diagonally across the intersection of Planique and Main, as he and Breed were waiting for the red DONT WALK signal to change.

It was the shank of a November Saturday shortened by reversion to Standard Time. The last football game of the season had been played earlier out at the stadium (without benefit of John's eyes and cheers), and the crowd was pouring back into the town and onto the campus. Potentially raucous singing could be heard echoing off the walls of the Forrestal Complex, and girls' laughter, too, scandalized, coquettish. Wagner had just gone bulling by, staggering home from the locker rooms, pie-eyed on powerful emotions, for he had won his letter and helped lose the game. As the two waited, the sidewalk across the way seemed a sensuous autumn garden, where pennants grew, loud knitted scarves, bronze chrysanthemums in buttonholes, souvenirs dangling from purple ribbons. One could hear many shouts—plans for fun.

From out of the crowd on the far corner the girl seemed to leap forward into John's attention: silhouetted against the window of the Sheldon Book Co-op, talking with two undergraduates, her head three-quarters averted from John's direction, light hair pinned up above a brown duffel-coat hood, no scarf, apparently no stockings, or at least not that season's dark meshed ones; an impression, without even a sight of her face, perhaps from the way she raised a hand to give it some eloquence, of fragility, vagueness, yielding.

Nearly a week had passed since the signing of the contract, and nothing had changed. John was still John. No experiences of any kind, to say nothing of breakthroughs. He had begun to waver between feeling cheated and wondering, with a roller-coaster plunge in his guts, whether, after all and all, Breed *had* been pranking. Just now he had realized that he had been waiting for Breed to make some move, and that perhaps Breed, to the contrary, had been expecting initiative from him.

The lights changed. Green WALK. The mass of students, who set much store by being casual, unregimented, and "free" in so many other aspects of life, were astonishingly docile in their obedience of the traffic lights; they began at once to walk, some with dates, across all four street throats, and catercorner, too.

On the way over, John grasped Breed's arm (brief thought of old Orreman), and said: —— There's a dame over there in front of the Co-op—

And broke off. Her head had turned. The face, from that now diminishing distance, came at John, as if by

zoom lens, and on the strength of what he saw he said to
Breed quickly, almost fiercely: —— Yes. She'd be a good
place to begin.

—— Which one?

—— That one with the brownish-blondish hair. With
the hood gadget. By the Co-op window.

—— Talking to those two ghouls?

—— With two guys, yes! You see her?

Still steering Breed by the arm, John stepped up on
the far curb and pushed through the eddies of men and
couples straight toward the Co-op window. The girl was
in the act of turning. Her hair was fine-textured, pinned
up every which way, with wisps flying. John and Breed
walked close by her, swiveling heads toward her, and
John saw, in her dropped eyelids and a moment of looking as if she had never been stared at in this world, that
she was plenty self-aware.

As soon as they were well away, John said (conscious that his voice might tremble): —— You made
promises to me.

Breed: —— O.K., don't blow a gasket. I suggest you
get lost for half an hour, then be at your room. I'll try to
have word for you then. These things aren't always so
easy.

For a while as dusk spread (how long had it taken to
walk out to Humblesmith that morning?), John strolled
on flagstones that seemed to be made of foam rubber.
Stripped elms, Gothic arches, the carillon tower, couples
arm in arm—Sheldon looked, for once, just great! Crisp
air with the faintest fragrance of burnt furnace oil. . . .

The chimes announced four forty-five. With no idea
how much time had passed, John hurried to his room.

In the card frame on his door John found a folded
note.

Her name is Margaret Gardiner. She's a townie.
She will expect a phone call from you at 229-5264
(home) at 5 p.m. Don't do anything Auld Hornie
wouldn't do! Word to the wise: I gathered Mom and
Pop may be rather strict.

John called from a glass outdoor booth on the corner
of Planique and Ash.

—— Hello?

—— Oh hi there.

—— This is John Fist. I guess you knew I was going
to call.

—— I just got in. Whew. Gotta catch my breath.

—— I was wondering . . .

—— Sure, I'd *adore* it.

But then John realized he had no idea what to suggest.

—— What do you think? (Very lamely.) Shall we——
Long silence.

Then she, most agreeably: —— I know a cool place. I
mean if you care for a typical little old beat-up minute
steak. Thing is, it's right out at the west end. You know.
Like it's sort of out of bounds for the domes.

—— The?

—— Domes. The domes. That's what my girl friend
and me call the college boys. I mean we could be sort of
away from the *atmosphere* out there. If that's what you'd
like.

John began to wonder what he had gotten himself in
for. Little old beat-up minute steak! How could there be
such a thing as a breakthrough of the spirit over a minute
steak, or any of Breed's work, for that matter? Was this
going to be a silly cheerleader of a high-school girl, waving pompoms and doing the watusi on the sidelines of a
basketball court? . . .

53

But when John entered the Gardiners' front door (they lived in Wagakyl Knolls, the dowdy older middle-class part of town, in a clapboarded house which had seemed, as John had rung the doorbell, to consist mostly of vast reaches of empty front porch; the doorbell had proved to be a set of chimes which played the theme of a headache-remedy commercial John had heard on television) and particularly when John saw the girl again, he felt reassured—because what she was at a glimpse was easy. Easy in the best sense: not just to make out with, but serene, compliant, well-bathed, unstylish, soft-mouthed, and right out through the roof on the maturity charts. John was so braced by her looks that he wanted—for the first time in several years—to do a buck and wing, but Mrs. Gardiner was circling around him as if he were an upright lamp in a lamp store and she was going to consider very carefully before placing an order. Mom called Pop in to meet The Young Man. Pop had a screw-driver in his hand and was perspiring. Mom said with iron lips (and the buck flew out the window, the wing fell in the ashcan):

—— I want you in not later than ten, Peggot.

—— O.K., Mom. (Just like that. Matter of course!)

But when they were out in the street, this talented girl slipped her hand in the crook of John's arm and said:

—— Don't mind *them*. They're just nice comfy Republicans. I don't have to be in at any old ten.

They sat in a narrow booth-for-two and talked across a linoleum-topped table in a greasy-spoon kind of place with a brilliant chrome jukebox Select-O-Matic head sticking out from the wall eavesdropping on every word they said. She did not seem silly at all; in other words, she asked about him. Wanted him to begin at the beginning. Her eyes had an incredible sparkle to them. He took a

beer, she drank ginger ale. On the jukebox the Rolling
Stones sounded as if they were trying to roll bricks. John
felt plunged into comfort with Peg, as he was soon calling
her (she said she loathed being called Peggot), but he
realized that at root nothing had changed, that he was
shy, dissatisfied, really in the same old slow-burning eternal rage. He told her what a disappointment Sheldon College was, he told her about Orreman's D—how the
pompous old professor *used* him so as to feel once again
his power over the generations of the unformed, over father and son.

Where the hell was the magic—the Klingsor trickery
Breed had promised? The music seemed to mock his
mood—Bob Dylan, the Animals, Jody Miller, the
Byrds. . . .

All these colleges, he said (echoes in his voice—
Gutwillig? Breed?), were really exploiting their students,
putting them through the old conformist success-
chopper.

But Peg wanted to know more humble things—about
his family, his home—and John suddenly found himself
praising his mother. A marvelously quick sense of humor,
he heard himself say. Phi Bete at Ogontz College—B.A. in
three years. Half Scotch Presbyterian extraction, half
Dutch Calvinist, a Katinka of the lochs, John said; her
Scottish side was the strong side, which made her sensuous, satin-cheeked, full of a gesturing vibrancy. She
chipped the air with her hands when she talked, made
wonderful shapes with flying fingers. Of the three children he was her favorite—he knew that. As he talked
John had a growing sense (beneath the talk, and not
heard in it) of his mother's strength: holding him in a
loving hug in such a way that he cannot move his arms.
She is crushing him! He thought (beneath the talk) of a

terrible letter he had read a few days ago, which Baudelaire wrote his mother, asking for money: *The harm is done through your imprudence and my mistakes. We are evidently meant to love each other, to live for each other, to end our lives as honorably and peaceably as possible. And yet . . . after my death it is obvious that you will not go on living. I am the only thing that keeps you alive. . . .*

—— She sounds just great.

—— She is—she's a very emotional person. (But the fervor was gone; that "emotional" could be understood two ways.)

They ordered the touted Breakthrough Steaks, and she asked where he lived.

Worcester. Edge of Worcester. His mother would have said "edge" like that—sounded like worthwhile suburbs. He told about the house with the glass wall.

His mother was restless, he told Peg, his father wanted to stay put in that house. His mother was always ragging his father, John said, to get out of old stick-in-the-mud New England, move to a frontier, some place where what you *did* was what mattered, not who you were. Or she would urge a summer—as if he could just pull up stakes anytime—on the Costa Brava, or in the Greek islands, when they came into fashion. . . .

—— Costa Brava (she said), where's that?

Watching Peg eat gave John a most unusual pleasure, one in which there was a strong current of anticipation. Her hands were so fluent; her hunger so open. Breed had written the word townie—his scorn of everyone and everything. She was in Sheldon Township High School, she told John, but John felt that he himself, in terms of Worcester, had been a townie of that town, he felt the kinship of rawness, unsophistication, with Peg.

But then, seeing a glaze of heavily creamed coffee on Peg's lips as she put her cup down, then licked the moisture away, he had a heady sense of her being experienced far beyond her years, and of her permissiveness—anything would go with her; yet she seemed completely and inviolably innocent, too.

John: —— What about your people? What does your old man do?

—— You saw them. (She shrugged—meaning, without special offense: ugh, one's parents.) Pop works for Zirko-Fuller. (Adding, seeing the emptiness in John's eyes:) Valves.

John let things rest there, with thoughts that Pop, screwdriver and all, had looked like an up-from-the-ranks executive, and that there were hints of laid-away substance in that house with the porch as big as all Nebraska; and suddenly he changed course.

—— Do you know many men from the college? (Realizing that he had put quite a load on "know" and on "men"; realizing he wasn't sure he wanted her to answer at all.)

But she was adroit: —— There's a few I enjoy talking with.

That held him. She had delivered that last line, giving him no answer at all, with a cheery, guileless, co-operative glint in her eyes. He felt encouraged—to give her joy by talking.

—— I had a sort of affair with this girl in high school (he was astonished to hear himself say), Madeline Turk was her name. . . .

Why in the world had he brought her up? Affair? Awkwardly John went on to say that he and Madeline had fancied themselves as movie buffs; he was too embarrassed to add that they had seen most of their classic films

57

at the Sunday-night meetings of the Youth Group of St. Luke's Episcopal Church.

—— Ever see *The General,* Buster Keaton? You didn't? Oh, that was really the greatest. This one scene— he's kissing his girl, see, with that sad Buster Keaton look on his face, they're standing by the drive wheels of a locomotive, and some of his soldiers come up to report, so he salutes to acknowledge them, but he's still glued to the girl, kissing her. . . .

John found great pleasure in imprinting aspects of himself on Peg, trying himself out on her, putting a narrated kiss, a very funny one, on her pliant moist lips.

Then he was talking about his grandfather:

—— . . . the gentlest and yet the strongest man I ever knew. Completely honest. We took this trip, my father couldn't go but *he* was along, down to Cuba—don't worry, it was before Castro, I was only about twelve. . . .

So now he was pouring out the Varadero memories: Why? The caves of Bellamar, the string of light bulbs, the section called Tiger's Throat, the guide, unable to pronounce "h," saying: —— We are calf way to the end; Gramps organizing a pig roast on a fire of mangrove wood, buzzards soaring overhead along Hicacos Peninsula; shells on French Beach: *Fissurella* ("Chinese hats," Gramps called them), *Pecten* ("fans"), *Donax variabilis* ("wings"), *Tellina* ("sunrise"); Gramps feeding iguanas *fruta bomba* rind by the public road through the du Pont place. Why was he telling all this?

Then he knew. He was leading up to the visit with Gramps to the rickety museum in Cárdenas: the rooms downstairs with historical mementos of the region, complete with the hero Rojas' chamber pot; and endless tables bearing a million miniature artifacts (a tiny Coke bottle, a tiny *Reader's Digest*)—and then the old "cura-

tor," who had been painting bird perches on the second
floor and wanted to point out *everything:* the fetus of a
goat with eight legs, in an enormous jar; a stuffed ele-
phant (poisoned by mistake in circus in *mil noveciento
veintitrés*); stuff bird, is call Zum, essmallest bird in
whole world, *treinta y cinco* centimeters from beak to end
tail. And then, John said:

—— He picked up this coin, said it was Roman, very
rare. It had these embossed figures on it, a naked man and
woman, having intercourse—doing it dog fashion. Been
at it for centuries.

Peg's hands flew to her cheeks. To his extreme annoyance, John felt himself begin to blush. He cursed his
own boyish beating around the bush, ending in this
blatancy. Was *this* getting down to the hardpan bottom
of reality? Breed's work? John wondered: Why haven't
I mentioned Breed to her?

But then he heard her saying, hands back down on
the tabletop.

—— There's a motel we could go to. (She was blushing now.) I don't mean tonight, I mean I'd have to sort of
set it up to be out for the night. I could let you know.
They say it's real nice—real modern. Sort of typical. I
mean I've only *heard* about it.

John had a bad moment of thinking that Breed had
put her up to this—rather than its being her idea, her
desire. John didn't want to ask her how she would arrange this with her ten-o'clock parents—he didn't want to
hear her lies. Any more of her lies. *Only heard about it!*

—— That would be great (casually).

Could she be weeping? Those *were* tears forming in
her eyes. Was she so movable and so moved? John
reached out a hand and covered one of hers on the table:
small, warm, and soft!

—— Excuse me just a sec (withdrawing her hand from under his).

She put both hands to her face, to one eye after the other. John heard slight sucking sounds. Then she put two little transparent cups on the linoleum by her coffee saucer. Contact lenses.

—— I just got 'em. Aren't they cool? Only thing is, you have to get used to them, they irritate your eyes at first—they make me start crying like a baby. But I just *love* 'em. Dr. Serle says they won't bother me for long.

Peg slipped her hand back under John's. The sparkle was gone from her eyes.

8

IN the next few days John felt himself in a battle with
time. He had once had a Yo-Yo, and had spent a month
perfecting many eccentric gyrations with it; and now the
hours behaved like that wooden Yo-Yo head—flying
down to the end of the string, slowly climbing back, veer-
ing, lazing in mid-air, staggering, tripping, then hanging
inert. John swung from a state of expectancy to one of
extreme boredom and back again. He stayed up all night
twice playing bridge with Breed and Wagner and Gibbon
(recalling that Grandma Newson, that sensuous puritan,
his mother's mother, wife of the best man in the world
and herself the biggest bitch of all time bar none, used to
refer to the deck, as she shuffled it with clicking crimson

fingernails, as the devil's picture book; she wouldn't play on Sundays). He slept till noon, till four. He would eat a snack at a drugstore in midafternoon, a huge meal at Emil's at midnight; skipped classes some days, went punctually and fully prepared on others. He beat the clock with endless arguments; light and dark became states of mind, not periods. He worked all one weekend, and took a Wednesday off.

There was no zest or even fury in all this. He was just waiting—for what, he scarcely thought about. Revelations? The Apocalypse? Something Breed would somehow arrange? To hear from Peg? He did drop by the post office rather often.

One afternoon, walking back to the Painter Complex from the library, where he had slept much of the afternoon in a leather armchair in the cool cave of the Sheldoniana Reading Room, he ran into a fellow named Lusk, whom he had met a couple of times with Breed, a tall gaunt graduate student who was "doing" comparative philology; he was a member of the Gutwillig crowd, and he was earning his way through graduate school—handsomely, they said—by preparing mimeographed portfolios of various professors' lectures (gathered for him in previous years by squads of eager beavers who knew shorthand) and selling them at high prices to students to save them the trouble of going to classes and taking notes. He had also written and set up an excellent handbook of shortcuts and dodges—e.g., how to satisfy the Sheldon minimum science requirement by combining Pier's Stonehenge (Anthrop 124, ½ cred, fantastically easy marker), Satterthwaite's Fruit Flies (Biol 26, lectures only, attendance not kept, ½ cred, instant sex among the decayed pears), and Plunger's Basic Rocks (Geol 20, 1 cred, freshman-level hardening of the earth crust, boring but the definitive gut); the whole point being to pass painlessly through Sheldon without any contact whatsoever with the repulsive discipline that had produced the Bomb, toxic insecticides, and an air-pollution index of 17.6 over You-Name-the-City. Lusk spent most of his time with undergraduates. He liked younger men—not in a queer way, as far as one could tell, but apparently because he enjoyed being with clever people whom he could outwit and exploit. He wore horn-rimmed glasses and had wild dirty curly hair. Though very skinny, he seemed completely impervious to weather, and even now at the end of November was walking in the street in chinos and a thin khaki shirt.

—— Hey, been looking for you. Chum tells me you've quit going to old Oval Ears' lectures.

—— Yeah, God yes (flattered by Lusk's having remembered this, considering that there were twenty-nine hundred undergraduates to keep track of).

—— Told me you said it was too far to walk.

—— It is! (Carried away.) Out to Humblesmith? For that shallow old fake?

—— Some reason! Eureka, that's tops. Listen, I've got the complete set of Orreman. (Voice lowered, an over-the-shoulder look like that of a peddler of erotica.) Only thirty dollars, you can have the whole works for thirty. We charge fifty to most guys.

—— No, no, no. I've quit Orreman altogether. I don't want any part of him.

—— Not just too far to walk, then? All right. (Crisply, regretfully admiring.) I accept that. Look, why'n't you come over to Forrestal for supper tonight? I saw Breed and I think he's coming. Spinter'll be there. Faglio. Maybe one or two others.

Gutwillig boys. Dom Faglio, whom John had also

63

met once or twice with Breed, had been to Mississippi on the Summer Project during the long vacation, and Spinter was the wild anti-organization Organization Man. John, telling himself that he wanted to see what the famous Spinter was like, accepted. . . .

They sat, the five of them, at the end of one of the long tables in the Forrestal refectory. Spinter turned out to be fiercely handsome, with a sharp eye-beam on which it was impossible to fasten for long, for fear of being slit, gutted, de-balled, salted, and laid out to dry. In dress he was casual and clean—rather more clean than casual. He was full of Gutwilligness. He was taking Faglio nastily over the coals, and John quickly felt himself siding with Faglio without particularly agreeing with his ideas (while in the background thoughts of Margaret Gardiner played, like Muzak, an inappropriate warm obbligato to his rather testy but poorly concentrated response to Spinter—a very queer two-leveled state: boredom and repulsion, anticipation and goose-pimpled buttocks).

—— You can't live by two rights (Spinter was saying in his sub-professorial snort-voice). All this effort in the Freedom Schools, teaching them our values. They'll passively accept what you say when you're face to face, and then shed it the minute your back's turned. There are two rights here, along with all the wrongs—a Negro right and a white right. You can't put 'em in the same noggin.

Faglio, a short, muscular Christian with dark circles under his eyes, could mutter, from all his passionate affirmative beliefs, only this gargled argument: —— Who told *you* what we teach in the Freedom Schools?

And yet these two, John thought, were closely allied under the Gutwillig intellectual umbrella—saw each other *all the time*, seemed to need each other, like a pair of symbionts, in order to survive at Sheldon.

64

Lusk raised his sharp face toward Spinter and said:
—— Four years ago around here it was nothing but Gins-
berg and Corso and Ferlinghetti, the next year it was all
atman and The Middle Way, then last spring it was Mc-
Comb and Ruleville and Holmes County. You know,
Spin, the trouble with going whole hog for one of these
nutty cults—or with *opposing* it whole hog, for that
matter—is that there's always some wise bastard in the
vicinity (a nod toward little Faglio) who knows more
than you do about it.

But this laugh-edged rebuke did not reach Spinter at
all; he took it, indeed, for a rebuke to Faglio. He said:
—— Ach, you can't choose a commitment any more: the
commitment chooses you, just grabs you. Last summer
(to John, who had the only new ears around) I was working out at Michigan on some research on autistic kids,
and I began to wonder: should I envy Dom Faglio being
down in Mississippi? Then I'd think, what the hell, there
really isn't any choice any more. You just fumble by accident into what you do. Don't you agree?

Spinter was asking *him*. He saw the harpoon of
Spinter's glance flying straight at his forehead. He ducked
just in time and said without enthusiasm (Muzak still
going): —— Oh, I don't know. (*Very* conscious of Breed.
How far short this fell of doing Breed's work!) I'm about
to have to choose a major. I guess there's a willful choice
of some kind there: it's a preliminary career choice, I
guess. I don't know if I can make it, but I've got to try,
anyway.

At this mild, inoffensive statement Spinter became
frenzied. He lit into John with a vehemence so great that
John could do nothing but blink his eyes, as if to adjust to
a sudden too-bright light. Spinter said he wished the college would eliminate the major—in fact, he was thinking

of starting a campaign through the Student Freedom Union to force the deans to abolish the major altogether. A student had a right to keep things open, not be fenced in. He has a perfect right to opt for a tentative identity—in fact, this is one of the *basic* student rights. The major-studies system is in direct violation of that right. It's deep in the American grain that a man must have the freedom of the next step. Majors! Jesus! That's what the whole thing hinges on!

Mild now was the word for John. Way down underneath, the Muzak was now set to words: I can't take this b.s. But outwardly John just muttered agreeably: —— I guess you have a point there.

This acquiescence cooled Spinter off, indeed made him act as if he were suddenly very fond of John, a newly discovered disciple, and John was surprised at being pleased by this adoption.

But after the meal, when Spinter asked John to come back to his room, along with Faglio, John had no hesitation in making an excuse—and as he and Breed walked away from Forrestal under street lights filtered through stark maple twigs, he began to develop a slow burn. As they walked his jaw muscles gnawed at things he should have said to Spinter. Finally he burst out:

—— Let's take off. God! I've *had* this horrible college.

—— Take off?

—— Let's (the huge charge suddenly draining off) take a walk.

—— I know a wizard place for a stroll. (Breed, affecting a British accent, sounded on the edge of a chortle, and John's anger began to build again.) The town dump. Charming by night.

. . . . They stood on a plateau of trash that was en-

croaching, like a lava bed, on a swamp by a bend of the
river to the south of town. Before them gaped the mouth
(into which a truck could drive) of the community in-
cinerator, a great metal cone with a wire-mesh hood, and
within, throwing up into its fierce convection a jubilee of
sparks and glowing paper ashes, burned the rage and
folly of yesterday's news, and heaps of what had been
designed as enticing packaging for market shelves, and
feasts of thrown-out leftovers, fatty chop bones not given
to dogs and crusts of bread left by spoiled children—a
holocaust of waste.

John was really in high, now that, on the way here,
he had poured out what he thought of Spinter, and he
was crazily intoxicated by the sight of this fire-lighted
outdoor museum of rusty auto engine blocks and mis-
shapen pots and cogs and drums. There was a crushed
bed frame! Nest of how many winters of love-making
under warm covers?

John, gazing back into the flames: —— Shit, Chum,
this is our old Protestant Hell. You know, I was brought
up on Milton's Puritan version of you: someone who could
build fires like that one—frugality, asceticism, individual-
ity, cruel righteousness, all in flames and smoke. . . .
Isn't that a smell of burning hair?

Breed, calmly: —— Mattress, I guess.

John: —— They sent me to Sunday school. You
know, it was my mother who insisted on switching from
Presbyterian to Episcopalian—pure social climbing. King
James's English, prayer-book elegance, that was what she
said she wanted me to learn: . . . *and thy presses shall
burst out with new wine . . . and our mouth shall show
forth thy praise . . . and show ourselves glad with psalms
. . . and upon the lute; upon a loud instrument, and upon
the harp . . .* Good phrases and good manners. Nothing

really about the soul, or about living and dying well, or about fires like this. It was my bitch grandmother—*she* didn't leave the Presbyterians—it was she who taught me about Hell. Hers and Calvin's. Endless writhing in the struggle between initiative and guilt. *From Greenland's icy mountains* . . . to these flames.

Breed: —— What's eating you, pal?

John: —— You. You. When do we begin?

Breed: —— *We?* Is it up to me?

John: —— When?

Breed: —— In the Boss's own good time. Cool, son.

9

How vivacious she was! She walked here and there inspecting the shabby motel room, moving with the stylized sashay of a model on a fashion-show ramp, pointing out to John with exaggeratedly ladylike gestures a funereal color print of a vase of calla lilies, a chest of drawers with a cracked glass top, walls of composition board with rows of nailheads showing under lemon-yellow paint, and, at the heart of the matter, a double bed (John could barely look at it) with a tufted green chenille coverlet. And a television set, on a wheeled stand.

—— Zenith. (In an airy voice, waving her hand drippingly over the machine.)

She bent and switched the TV on. When the image

came on with a roar, she turned the volume down to silent but left the picture flickering.

She wheeled and, draping herself against the bulky set as if she were a night-club singer leaning back on a piano, said:

—— Our little home. Our little unsplit-level home.

John laughed and moved toward her.

She whirled away as if waltzing and went into the bathroom. Her voice came out tile-hardened and echoing:

—— *Désastre! Il n'y a pas un bidet!* (Then a reverberating giggle—was it over her touristy accent or her little worldly-wise joke?)

She poked her head out of the bathroom door and said:

—— How'd you like our friend who signed us in? Wasn't he right out of the Munsters?

The man in the motel office (John had felt immensely relieved that it had turned out to be a man) had been sitting in a swayback sofa, with a very old asthmatic collie at his feet, watching television. An electric clock on the wall had said it was nine-twenty. On sensing the presence of John and Margaret, the man had made no effort to rise, but turned his face, with two huge purple bags under the eyes, toward them, without, however, tearing his gaze from the tube.

—— Commercial be right on. You don't mind holding your horses a couple of minutes, do you?

This was not a situation in which John felt he could object to a proprietor's rudeness. At last Viceroy cigarettes took over, and the man heaved himself up. He was wearing an old green buttoned sweater. He was absurdly lugubrious. Perhaps on purpose he never looked at these children's faces; he watched John's hand as it wrote: *Miss*

Cynthia Doggett. John signed just a girl's name, according to Margaret's instructions.

—— Rather have double or twin?

John, going along with the act Margaret had outlined: —— Doesn't matter to you, does it, Cynthia? I mean, you're the one who'll be—

He broke off, having no taste for pretense that no one took for real.

Margaret, easily: —— Make it double.

The man sighed deeply, as if for the ruin of a whole generation, and said, seeming to have memorized the dry, euphemistic instructions: —— In case of occupancy by two parties, the rate will be twenty-one dollars. Pay now. Rebate of seven dollars if one party leaves.

John, knowing it was a holdup, nevertheless paid docilely, almost eagerly. He saw the man's eyes watch the delicate trembling of the bills as he reached them out. The sad old man handed John an old-fashioned straight key. . . .

Now Margaret came out of the bathroom. She patted the bed. Then she pulled the chenille bedspread down from the pillows and right off the bed, and she folded it, tucking the edges under her chin, spreading her arms wide for each new fold. John had the feeling, as he watched this breezy transaction, that she was playing house—playing motel. She seemed utterly innocent; her sophistication was put on, almost caricatured.

—— Getting used to your contact lenses?

—— Oh, you can't really tell whether I have them on.

—— Yes, I can. They just don't look like real eyes, that's all.

—— Phooey to you.

John remembered getting her letter arranging all

71

this: He had gone through the college post-office arcade late the previous Wednesday morning, after a class, and on opening his box he had found three envelopes: a letter from his mother, a bill from the undergraduate-managed clothes-cleaning service, and a pale-green envelope with a local postmark, on the address of which the point over the "i" in Fist was a small circle with a dot inside it. He had put his mother's letter and the bill back in the box, had slammed the little metal door shut, and, still bent down, had worked a forefinger under the flap of the green envelope when suddenly he saw the absurdity of the picture—*he*, snatching open a letter while still hunched down over a mailbox. He straightened up, put the letter in his pocket, and got as far as the sidewalk before he took it out, opened it, and, standing at a curb, greedily read it.

She had thought of everything: a meeting away from her house to jibe with her story to her parents, proposal of an out-of-the-way diner for an inexpensive supper, name and address of the motel (she had suggested a cab, but in the end John had borrowed Breed's car), suitcase for her but none for him, what to say and do when they got to the motel. There was no nonsense in the letter, no archness, no wavering. John had had an instant's imaginary glimpse of Breed dictating this straightforward language to her, and at that thought his soaring exuberance had become tinged with anger; but he had rejected everything about that bitter idea except the realization that this letter, with a little bull's-eye over each "i," had a definite air of experience about it, which John liked and didn't like.

She sat on the foot of the bed, kicked her shoes off, and looked at the soundless snowy blinking of the television screen, and for a brief moment her expression grew bleak.

John, still standing like a post not far from the door, said what he least wanted to say: —— How often have you done this?

The question, strangely enough, drove the winter from Margaret's face, and with a look of renewed gaiety and irony she stood up and walked straight toward John, raising her hands as she approached him, as if offering him something. That something turned out to be—as he, realizing it, opened his arms to receive it—an embrace. Her hands went higher yet, and she lay her weightless forearms on his shoulders. They kissed.

He felt what seemed to him a practiced hand at the back of his neck. (Or was that palm so sure of itself? Or was this something she had seen done in movies? Or was she just a natural?) She wore no lipstick; he had never had a lipstickless kiss before—for Madeline had worn dark-red and, last year, silver lipstick; and all the other casual mouths around Worcester had been cerise, or white, or cherry-petal, or some "new" shade. These lips seemed undressed. In the very moment of remembering the question he had asked just before this happened (how often for her?) John realized the question was blurring in his mind; it didn't matter, he could forget it. He sensed that he was taking the initiative, his arms moved, he held her body tight against his.

Then, altogether in charge, feeling that whatever might happen would be best if he didn't rush things, he pulled back and said: —— How about let's have a Coke? I saw some vending machines over next to the office.

—— Wait a minute, hon.

Hon, indeed! Where could she have picked up such an endearment as that? Did Mrs. Gardiner of the iron lips use that word speaking to Pop? Margaret clicked the catches of her suitcase, flipped open the top, lifted out a hairbrush, and took a gentle swipe at his cowlick, which had fallen partway forward during the hug. John felt like a husband being sent off to the office—and quite capable, too, of handling the day's business.

He was back soon with a couple of Cokes and a cardboard bucket of ice cubes.

For a moment John had a queer feeling that he had walked into the wrong room. A girl was on the bed, propped up against the headboard, a pillow wedged behind her back and shoulders, with her arms raised and her hands behind her head. The lifting of her arms and shoulders had pulled her skirt partway up her thighs. One leg lay crossed over the other. She seemed not to be Margaret though.

Then he saw why: She had unpinned her hair and brushed it out, and it hung now about her neck and shoulders. She seemed more demure now, and subdued.

He peeled off his jacket, pulled his tie loose, and unbuttoned his shirt collar; poured the Cokes and sat on the other side of the bed from her.

Margaret: —— What do you want to be?

John, lightly, responding to a very strong recurrence of the feeling that they were playing house: —— You mean when I grow up?

She laughed at that and nodded her head.

—— I'm in a kind of a bind about that at this point. I don't even know what I'm going to major in next year.

As John talked, Margaret gazed at the fitful pictures on the silent television tube, but he could tell that she was listening to him: he seemed to be the soundtrack for a harrowing but mute doctor-drama. He told her about the arguments you could hear any night of the week in the Painter Complex about Opting the Right Career.

—— These guys split hairs about making a commitment till they sound like a bunch of lawyers at a murder trial. There's a kid named Faglio—I call him a kid, hell,

74

he's my age easily, it's just that he's a kidlike individual—
he was in Mississippi last summer. Everything's so simple
for him, so clear. I wouldn't mind trading places with
him—I don't mean right this minute!

John patted her thigh in what started as a casual
gesture of reassurance: he wasn't going to go up in
smoke, leaving the stubby figure of Dom Faglio in his
stead on the edge of the bed. But the touch of his palm on
her resilient flesh, so near the mound of Venus (its shape
visible where the soft cloth fell in folds around it), made
him draw in his breath. Quickly her eyes left the TV and
turned to his, with a look of swift interrogation. John
drew back into fast talk.

—— Dom's not like most of your civil-rights fanatics.
Most of them get so superior—if you haven't *been*, as
they say, why you just aren't anybody. One thing gripes
me: They keep talking about how marvelous the experience was for *them*.

—— I know what you mean (Margaret said, her eyes
back on the scene in the operating amphitheater). Other
day on this transistor I have, I heard a plug for the Peace
Corps, and it sounded exactly like an Anacin commercial.
Are you tense? Neurotic? go to Uganda, that throbbing in
your head will vanish. . . . Not a word about the Ugan-
dians—or Ugandans—which *is* it?

—— Professor Gutwillig says . . .

Again the questioning eyes came away from the set,
and John noted sourly that the unknown name had
brought much the same look as the pat-caress on her
thigh.

—— Gutwillig's a hotshot in sociology, he's sort of an
all-purpose whiz. He says all these activities are just role-
playing. You try on a Mississippi mask one summer, then
a poet mask or a stevedore mask or an office-boy-for-the-
Kansas-City-*Star*-with-a-vague-idea-of-going-into-govern-

ment mask the next summer. This way there's no such thing as committing yourself, it's just a personality act, a game of parts—like *The* Game. You know, that charade thing where you pick up sides. . . .

—— Sure, we used to play it all the time. That, and In the Manner of the Adverb. Ever play—

—— You learn the signals, you know, how to get things over real fast, and the only trick is to *let yourself go* on each title, or slogan, or saying, or quote, or whatever it is you're acting out. That's more or less the Gutwillig theory on careers. Only it comes out that if you choke up, if you're scared of a role, you're really scared of yourself.

Margaret had been watching John's mouth since she had spoken. Now she looked back at the set (John decided she just liked seeing things move) and said: —— I know a fellow, he's a junior in the college, and he's got it all taped. He knows what he wants. Real career-hound. He knows exactly what's going to happen at every stage—how much he'll earn the first year, the fifth year. . . . You can't get him to give an opinion: couldn't possibly get him to say whether he was for L.B.J. or Barry. He won't risk everything he's lined up so carefully by any such foolishness as having an opinion about anything *controversial*.

John was taken aback by this, Margaret's first mention of another student, and he found he smartly didn't like it, even though she had seemed to be deriding the man's attitude. John was silent awhile, hoping she would register that he was—what?—uncomfortable? But she sat serenely studying the jumping shadows in the machine.

John suddenly broke out: —— I don't want to be fenced in! This majoring business. With all the variety that college has to offer, you ought not to be forced to make a choice in your second year.

John was burning, but all traces of his anger at Spinter seemed to have disappeared. Here he was, practically quoting Spinter. Next thing he'd be out carrying a placard against the deans.

Margaret said with sudden conviction: —— Education's been copped by the roaches and rats.

There was a talk game going around that autumn called Slogans—quick exchanges of catch phrases of mock doom—and now the one that Margaret had just uttered triggered off a flurry of them:

He: —— Sign up and knuckle under.

She: —— Napalm the fruggers.

—— Yeah, draft 'em—they're old enough to kill but not to vote.

—— Abandon ship! Men first in the lifeboats, women second, children last.

John was completely at peace again. This girl was so agreeable, so compliant—but he had the impression that she knew exactly who she was, and that there was a little of her mother's iron under the softness. He set the odd pillow against the headboard and stretched out on the bed parallel to her.

In time, of course, they got around to talking sex—in books—and again John had a hard time figuring out just where Margaret stood. She had read all the standards, it developed, as he dropped the names. *Naked Lunch, Candy, Last Exit to Brooklyn*, Miller, Mailer. What was *this* coming from those lipstickless lips?

—— . . . more orgasms to the paragraph than any other writer living or dead. . . .

John asked if she liked Genet.

—— Well, I *know* about him (slight frown in the direction of the inaudible late news). My girl friend showed me a book of his, something about flowers, *Saint*

77

of the Flowers? Not quite that, something like that, but I can't stand all that faggy stuff about peeling your rectum right back over your whole body. It makes me really oops, that kind of image.

Liberation, sometimes called pornography by parental types, was in the air they breathed, along with CO_2 and the hydrocarbons and other possibly carcinogenic pollutants, but Margaret, John decided, simply inhaled and exhaled whatever blew past and remained completely free of toxication. She was *post*-liberated; she talked about these things as if they belonged to an older generation. Older people wrote those books for older people to read and throw up over. She was aware but she was untouched.

John felt a sudden pull, slightly unpleasant, toward further testing, and he glided into talk of devils and witches, and soon was saying: —— A friend of mine was telling me about how far Thomas Aquinas, I mean a great thinker like Aquinas, fell for witchcraft. He wrote perfectly seriously about how incubi and succubi would screw with humans, and sometimes they got sperm by milking fresh corpses by *fellatio.*

Margaret's hands flew to her cheeks, just as they had in the restaurant that other night, and then she said: —— Something's burning. Turn the TV off, there must be something gone in the idiot box. Smells like it.

Going to the set, John felt a sudden elation, a sense of power; then, with a chilling letdown, he realized he had never even mentioned Breed to Margaret. He thought perhaps he never would.

He lay down again and soon said in a chanting tone:

Chaque jour vers l'Enfer nous descendons d'un pas,
Sans horreur, à travers des ténèbres que puent.

78

Margaret said: —— Say that again slowly. I adore
French, it's my one not-weak point in school, but I have a
real slow ear.

He repeated the couplet.

—— *L'Enfer?*

—— Hell.

—— Oh God yes. Shadows that what?

—— Stink.

—— Ugh.

—— Every day we take one more step down toward
Hell, without horror, through vile-smelling shadows.

—— Yes, I got it the second time around; that's *beautiful*. But . . .

John realized he had expected her somehow to start
things—take off her clothes, come to him. But after her
"but" she began a delicious yawn. She let herself down
from the headboard, turned on her side facing him, drew
up her legs, and put both hands under her left cheek; she
looked utterly contented, utterly unspoiled. She was
searching his eyes now—looking perhaps for the flickering pictures of some silent story, an inner late late
show.

She said: —— You're a very nice man.

But this praise made him at once self-critical. He
began to blame himself for belittling everything. He
hated (he told himself, as he put it in different words to
Margaret) the nego in Breed, Spinter, Lusk. Why did he
display all the same bitter stuff himself? The more he
blamed himself, the more virtuous and praiseworthy he
felt: how sterling of him to be able to talk about his
shortcomings with such complete honesty!

She protested weakly: —— Oh, hon, you're not like
that.

He talked on. (He remembered that Madeline had

more than once called him on this self-loving self-hate of his.) After a few sentences he looked over.

Margaret was fast asleep.

He sat up, went to the door, and snapped off the overhead light, then stepped over and turned off the bathroom light; this left a reading lamp burning on his side table. By its glow he took the folded bedspread and gently covered Margaret. Then he crawled in on the other side, turned out the reading lamp, pulled part of the bedspread over himself, and fell sound asleep in an astonishing bath of happiness. He slept as still as a stone all night.

IO

By the next afternoon, John had gone into a big burn. His rage grew and grew. He knew very well that, according to something known as the New Morality, a person was not supposed to feel guilty over doing anything that was fun, and John, as a result, now felt furious compunction precisely over having done nothing at all. Damned for a do-nothing.

He was sore at everyone and everything, including Margaret, who, in the morning, in a blur of rumpled clothes and unbrushed teeth, had ruefully told him she was afraid she was awfully gone on him. He had dropped her off at ten o'clock at a movie house that was just open-ing, where she said she would kill time till she could make it home and make it plausible, too. How long had she stayed at that show—five or six hours?

She had asked when she would see him again. He had made no promises.

He was particularly angry, and grew more so as time passed, at Breed, who did not take the trouble to come around and ask how things had gone. John sought Breed out and lied to him—didn't exactly come right out and say that he had screwed the girl; but he did say he had slept with her. After that he just plain lied: said she was an enthusiast; went in mostly for seniors, collected them like charms on a charm bracelet; *hated* graduate students, said they were too poky and talky.

But John understood that Breed did not believe one word of it. Breed smiled—that gracious display of dental enamel of his, which suggested, beneath the generous eyes, an eternity of gnawing, biting, snapping, gnashing.

For a couple of days after that, John was jittery and jumpy. A sudden horn in the street would pour a bucket of anxiety over his neck and back; Flack looking over his shoulder in the mirror as he shaved in the morning made him jump so he cut himself; the sight of "My Tetralogy" lying among the papers on his desk, with Orreman's D, in a tremorous yet disciplined Palmer Method script, reproachfully leaping out at him, threw him into a real cold sweat.

Then everything seemed gradually to go flat and dull and boring, and John found himself wasting time on the damnedest pursuits—solitaire, which he hadn't played for years; walking by the hour (Humblesmith had seemed, one morning, he remembered, too far away to walk to); and bothering other guys when they were trying to work. The other shoe was on Wagner's foot now; John had a ball bothering Wagner, who was stuffy about studying now that he had his beloved sweater. John felt rather wistful, detached, during this time.

By the following Wednesday he realized he had stopped going to classes altogether. For good.

The only thing that worried him was that he wasn't worried. He felt no anger, no anything, it seemed, any more. Flack couldn't get a rise out of him; not even Spinter, whom he saw one night, could rile him.

All he had left in the way of feeling, he decided, was a resentment of being manipulated, as he constantly felt he was being, by Breed.

One night, very late, Breed began talking (he didn't *seem* to be suggesting a course for Fist) about mortification. He described the psychic states—the feeling of lightness, the extraordinary mental lucidity, the tonic silence, the teetering on the sill between the conscious and the subconscious—that came to one who practiced, to just short of excess, certain austerities: fasting, pain, lack of sleep. Breed recited the stories of anchorites, saints, Oriental mystics, famous ascetics: the supernatural powers they had seemed to acquire, their miraculous visions and insights.

John protested: —— *You,* giving me all this poop about holy men?

Breed, his eyes twinkling: —— Attaboy, keep up your suspicions. Don't trust me for a minute. *Daemoni, etiam vera dicentes, non sunt credendi.*

Yet what Breed was saying did seem credible—that by putting his self-indulgences under guard, by setting a cop out to curb his pleasures and bug his thoughts, one could whittle his perceptions to pierce deep, deep down, so he would begin to have waking dreams, hear whispered commands, penetrate the most difficult puzzles.

But the more believable all this seemed, the more

John drew back from it. He felt more and more like someone walking in a dark city street, alert to the possibility of being mugged and robbed.

The next day he sat at his desk and wrote:

Dear Mum and Father:

> *Don't faint. Just a note to let you know that everything is O.K. Can't say I'm setting any records but I'm doing all right for me. ~~Tell Dad~~ I have old man Orreman's lecture course, and I guess he may even be my favorite. Other subjects: industrial development in last half century (wildcat named Gutwillig teaches), trig—ugh, 19th-Cent. novel in England & Russia, and a thing on fruit-fly mutations in response to radiation for science requirement. About that island trip. I may be going skiing during the spring vacation so don't count on me. I met a girl I think even a guy's parents would like—might bring her home some weekend. In case you're wondering, at the moment I figure about a B-minus average. Well I have to run to a class now.*
>
> > *Your dutiful son,*
> > *John.*

He mailed the letter, too; but he neither ran nor walked to any class at all. It almost seemed too far to walk anywhere now.

BOOK TWO

II

—— Throw your clothes on the chaise longue, honey.

She made it sound a little like cheese lounge. He wondered if he would have a lifetime of girls who called him honey. The full word honey seemed to him a degree upgraded from, if perhaps a shade less feeling than, Margaret's plain hon.

So this was a whore. John was astonished by her. She was much younger than he had expected one would be, and she looked quite a lot like a Bennington girl he had met skiing the previous year. Could she be the self-same one, taking junior year off, on a one-woman, domestic-peace-corps-type project? No, she was slightly out of focus for a Bennington girl, and something was a bit funny with the audio, too.

87

But nice. She sat on the edge of the bed in a severe, chic gray suit, the gap between high fashion and the merchandise of the local women's store, Kahn's Modes, where she had quite possibly bought this, apparently consisting of no more than a difference in the scale and finish of buttons; hers looked like two rows of smallish pumpkin pies set out to cool. But other than buttonwise, as Wagner might have put it, she was terrific. Her career had not marked her face (he was not sure what he had expected: A vulcanized recapping job on the jowls and lips? A purple pure-foods-and-drugs stamp on her forehead?) and her skin was clear, transparent, and suffused with healthfulness, as if a nice cool *rosé* ran in her veins. Her hair was dark, straight, shoulder-length. When she talked he saw a glint of some metal that was not gold on one of her teeth. She was smoking a non-filter cigarette, and she inhaled to her very marrow, as if drinking from the fountain of youth.

He was at a loss what to do. Was he supposed to undress and perform with no preliminary amenities whatsoever? No clothed kisses? No gradual stimulation of erogenous zones during divestitive courtship as advocated in *Ideal Marriage* by Dr. Van de Velde, a cherished author of his fourteenth year? Was he to fling his clothes on the chaise longue, according to directions, without even getting to know her name? He had come for experience. In this long, slow, debilitating, fuse-burning time he had been going through, he had suddenly decided that rescue from his boredom and nervousness might come through action—through carrying his often-expressed credo (I believe in the divinity of the sense experience . . .) over into the realm of actuality. At last. He felt that one of his troubles must have been his lag, his being so far behind both his imagination and his generation, or, at any rate, concerning the latter, behind the talk he was forever hearing from big mouths like Ackercocke's and Gibbon's about what was supposed to be going on in the weenie factory. To get in the swim he would have to go in the water.

So here he was. He had very much not wanted Breed to know he was going to do this, and he had gone to Emil, the hash-slinger, for advice. Over scrambled eggs early one morning he had asked Emil in a low voice if Emil knew where he could get a good piece. He tried to sound as if this was an old question with him, but Emil, by the nature of his answer and the tone of its delivery, had made it clear that he knew a rookie when he saw one.

—— They got two kinds (Emil had said). You want fi-buck or twenny-buck poontang? You fancy Shel bastids lookin for big-time hunnerd-buck stuff, you can't get it roun here. They only got homemade hair pie roun here. You know which one you want, Shel, five or twenny? (Emil called all Sheldon men at his counter Shel.)

John had thought twenty sounded safer than five.

Emil had given him an address out in the west end (very close, it had turned out, to the breakthrough-minute-steak joint to which Margaret had taken him that first night), and had added:

—— I'd advise a Tuesday or Wensey. You don't run into no big rush hour them days, 'cause sometimes out to Mabel's they get 'em stacked up like Kennedy Airport, time you hit the deck you damn near outa fuel. It's the popalation explosion.

Mabel's. That name, and having gotten his advice from hostile Emil with his appalling apron and his horrible gargled expressions, had caused John to picture a desperately squalid setting, a redolence of stale malt and dead cigars, a prostitute in a drab, rumpled yellow sateen dressing gown with hems soiled from having been dragged across two decades of transactions with trailer-truck pilots and short-order potbellies like Emil. And now to find this little chintzy guest room, with what was surely a Steuben ash tray (gift from a Sheldon regular?) on a recently waxed wing-leaf coffee table, on which also reposed a late number (left by an absent-minded professor?) of *The Journal of Existential Psychiatry;* and this crisp off-Bennington girl dressed for an orgy of Tchelitchew and Warhol and Picasso at the Museum of Modern Art, pop-art buttons and all! John felt the haze of his depression thinning, for this was a splendidly pleasant surprise.

—— We cough up in advance here, honey. (A hand was floating in his direction, palm up.)

John reached with great haste for his wallet.

—— That's twenty?

—— For you it's twenty, darling. You see, it's safer to pay now; you might want to put up twice as much after. (A nice inviting smile, spiced by that tooth cap that wasn't gold.)

John handed her the money. She put the bills in the Steuben ash tray, stood up, and with disconcerting rapidity, bypassing those remarkable buttons altogether, unsnapped a single something and stepped out with one breasting motion into total nakedness.

John, who had never even seen a completely nude woman before, except on magazine pages and, fleetingly, in a Swedish movie, found a sudden new interest in these proceedings. She was terrific. Not a bruise on her. (The latest of his Emil-reactions.) He began hurriedly to undress. He shucked his jacket, shoes, socks, and trousers easily, but when he came to his shirt buttons he found that the ends of his fingers were numb. The woman

90

stepped close in front of him, pushed his hands aside, and shaking her head like a prim schoolteacher over some all-too-familiar classroom delinquency, unbuttoned the row from top to bottom; she remembered the sleeves, too. Then she turned her back and got a metal basin, rather hospital-looking, out of a cupboard and half-filled it with water from a large pitcher. When she faced him again, with the basin in her hands, he was in the altogether. And very interested in her.

—— What class're you in, honey? (Putting the basin down on the coffee table.)

—— Sophomore.

At that she swallowed. There didn't seem to be any particular force in her swallowing; it wasn't as if she were trying to keep from throwing up. She just swallowed as if she always did on hearing the word sophomore.

With a hand on his left buttock she firmly moved him closer to the coffee table and began to wash his privacy with a soap that smelled antiseptic; the water was warm.

—— Mmmm (she said). What a nice big boy.

And more so by the moment.

—— God (he said), it's like getting ready for an appendectomy.

—— You betcha. I took a course in practical nursing, honey. And that's the way I mean to keep it. Practical.

She rinsed him off and dried him with several Kleen-exes, giving his now militant selflet some very friendly pats and squeezes. She put the basin on the floor and carefully dried the few drops of water that had splashed on the coffee table.

Then quite suddenly she lay on her back on the bed, raised her knees, spread her legs, and beckoned to him in a startlingly genteel way with the tips of her fingers.

John presented himself. It was all very much as described in the literature. He kept his weight suspended over her, just as Dr. Van de Velde had so kindly suggested, on his elbows and knees. This girl who had no name assisted tactfully, dexterously, at his entrance at the gate of his dreams.

There! John lay quite still on her, snug as on eider down, thinking about how really pleasant this was. This was definitely a big moment in his search for sentience. Time seemed to float.

—— All right, honey, concentrate.

John remained immobile, steeped in thought. He was enveloped, he was one with her. Yet this was not, he knew, the fusion he desired. This partner was a total stranger; even here in this situation, having received him utterly, she was a stranger to him. How far apart they were, in this deep peace!

—— Look, darling (she said), put your mind on your homework.

But still he lay still. It was not that he was not excited. He was. His excitement, however, was largely philosophical. She was warm against him. She was an exceedingly friendly person, very helpful and understanding, and John felt washed with good luck. On this note of being blessed, his mind wandered from the room. Perhaps one of these days he might walk out to Humblesmith again—just to test the distance once more.

But now she spoke again, and this time her voice seemed edged by that glistening tooth cap:

—— Get cracking, Shel. The meter's running.

John roused himself, and to earthquakes of encouragement from beneath he came eventually and most pleasurably to the point. It was, he decided, upon separation and further reflection, an exceedingly fine experi-

ence, a delight of delights. . . . But not what he had
thought of as a breakthrough. Definitely not a psychic
breakthrough. Not yet Breed's reward, nor Breed's work,
either. But he didn't want to think of that!

She lit one of those filterless cigarettes. He lay beside
her.

—— Do you mind if I ask you something?

—— Look, honey, *please*, none of those social-studies
questions.

—— No, no. I just wondered if you'd mind telling me
your name.

But she ignored his query, being apparently quite
steamed up on the subject of post-orgasmic cross-exami-
nation.

—— These big respectable profs come in here, they
smell to high heaven of pipe tobacco, they always tell me
the reason they've come is they're celebrating getting on
tenure, see, or else they're celebrating keeping somebody
else off it, boy that tenure stuff is like Spanish fly, I mean
you just *say* the word tenure and nine out of ten of those
guys begin to lech around like wild animals, I mean
they'll bite your shoulder and no telling what they'll ask
you to try. So after they knock one off, then the quiz
begins. Multiple-choice questions, they want to know
about the oldest profession. It's always by them the oldest
profession. I feel like telling 'em teaching's pretty goddam
old, too, but there's no time for that, we've got this big
quiz going, all these questions about occupational motivation and socio-sexual variables. On the level, honey,
who should hand out the marks is me, not them.

This little tirade over, John, who was in a felicitous
vague haze of something like indifference, asked again for
her name. He felt he had a right to it now. She reached
over John, leaning heavily on him, and, flicking his dollars

aside with a finger, stubbed out her half-smoked cigarette.

—— My name? It's just Mona.

—— That's quite pretty (he said insincerely) if you listen to it for its sounds. Names mean a lot to me. Seems to me that names enter all the way into people and help shape them. You take a common name like Margaret. That comes from the Latin, *margarita,* meaning pearl. So every Margaret is a kind of a pearl, isn't she? There's a speck of grit or sand inside and the mother-of-pearl gets laid over it, till you have something quite beautiful in the end, all coming from that tiny bit of inner irritation. See what I mean?

—— Oh, honey, you in love? That why you came out to me?

—— God, no (speaking rather more vehemently than the context required). I just meant in general.

—— In general covers a lot of sins, baby. Those tenure sex fiends always start their questions with the words in general.

Mona raised herself on an elbow beside him, and she looked at him and said, as if seeing him for the very first time:

—— Hi. What's with you?

—— My name's John.

—— Names don't mean that much to me.

—— How can you tell who somebody is if you don't know his name?

—— Who says I want to know who he is? To me, you're a Shel. . . . Listen, baby, I want to ask *you* some questions. They're always coming in here and grilling me. Now *I* want some background information. O.K.?

John shrugged lying down. He was thinking how nice it was that Mona didn't have a heart of gold.

—— Look, dearie, I'll make a deal. You stay on with

me like say a half hour, and I can ask you anything I
want, and I'll pay you ten bucks for your time. Is that
fair?

—— Sure. What do you want to know?

But perhaps his response was too cool, too shaded by
the haze in which he hung, for she grew anxious:

—— You don't think that's a fair deal, is that it? You
want your whole twenty back? That it? It's all right with
me. Twenty.

—— No, Mona, hell, I don't want any money. Just
ask me.

—— Oh, so, money's good enough for me, is that it?
But *you* can't take money, not you. I mean you place
educated questions and common ordinary pussy in two
different categories, is that it? In general?

—— Ten would be very nice.

—— All *right*. First off, why do you go around so
sloppy? You can afford to look nice, why do you have to
look so slept-in? Look at that hair!

—— You sound like my mother.

—— Any woman would want to know.

—— Would you like the truth? I'd like to be cul-
turally deprived. The only people with real privileges
these days are the underprivileged. Listen, tenure is
anathema to me. I want to get off. They've got me aimed
straight for graduate school right this very minute. I've
had God knows how many years of getting into places. I
wouldn't take tenure if you gave it to me in gift wrap-
ping.

—— Oh, honey, don't get sore. I didn't think you
were one of those tenure beasts. I could tell from the way
you went at it you weren't one of *them*. You were real
sweet. Are you a virgin? I mean were you?

—— Uh-huh.

95

—— How could you be a virgin at your age?

—— I guess I was just so busy getting into college I didn't have time.

—— You ask me, I think they ought to do away with half the colleges. . . . Honey you were O.K. Just a matter of getting the motor started the first time. I'm sorry I hollered at you. You're going to be fine.

—— It's funny, I think I sort of dimly knew that about myself. I realize it must've been obvious to you that I didn't really know beans—not even Word One; but even though I've been feeling sort of funny lately, I think I knew I'd be O.K. in *that* part of it. I don't know, I just had an idea about it. But thank you for saying that, that was nice.

—— Look (in sharp tones), don't try to soap me up with any of that *nice* fluff. That word gives me the jingle-jangles. But listen, here's what I really want to know. What's eating you?

—— You mean in the sex department? You mean what would make a clean-cut boy like me come out here?

—— Watch your language. I mean in general. What the hell, do I have to put it to you in multiple-choice? What's the itch? You said you'd been feeling sort of funny lately—that's what I mean. It sure can't be funny-ha-ha. What *is* it? It's so *many* of you Shels like this.

—— Could I bum one of those ciggies?

And so for half an hour and ten bucks, John talked about everything except the central thing—everything but Breed. The deadness of most of the teaching, the pipe-smokers Mona detested (how any hint of respectability made her bristle!), all that publish-or-perish nonsense, the pile of postponements on his desk, Orreman and the D, horrible Flack, the long, long road to Humblesmith. And he suddenly began blurting out an account of his first girl, his pre-Madeline love—at the age of fourteen struck speechless by a certain Ginny; sitting on a bench under a maple tree one night outside the junior high while a dance was going on inside, at which the inordinately daydreamed-about Ginny was bopping with some frightful jerk, while he, on the bench, talked in a gruesome intimacy with a hated rival, Pat Donalson, a classmate, who thought Ginny was, as he put it, hot as cat spit, and they dwelt on her charms, particularly what they called her bazooms (slowly accreting then like two little hourglass cones of sand)—and now, recapturing that scene with this completely naked Mona beside him, John felt an absurd, shameful, and puzzling surge of tears in his eyes.

He stopped talking, muted by his effort to control this ridiculous mood.

Into the silence Mona plunged with a suddenly dirgelike voice that came from way down under that magnificent bosom of *hers:*

—— Someday I'll tell you about my first guy. He was a real rotten son of a booger. He put me right smack where I am today. I mean single-handed. Was he bad news! He had it made, honey, he was the son and heir of—oh croust, I better not get into names—but enough to say there was a Lincoln Continental in the picture, upstairs maids yet, all the whip cream you wanted . . .

As she talked on, John, freed from his own queer little attack of emotional vertigo, had a distinct feeling that this fine crazy whore was making up every word of her crappy yarn. He thought of doing a paper about her for Gutwillig. She had said "someday," which suggested a future.

Then, bong, he had a better idea. He would take her home for a weekend. He'd written about maybe bringing a girl home. He saw how really, really wonderful that would be.

He invited her with a flicker of wondering whether Breed had in some mysterious way put this idea in his head, and at once she said:

—— I'd love to, honey. That sounds like a real old-fashioned picnic. What did you say your name was?

12

BREED, his chin propped on a polka-dotted red bow tie, stood in the doorway.

—— I hear you've been gracing houses of ill-repute. Tisk tisk.

—— Brother. Some private life a guy has around here.

—— Clue Emil and you've put it in the papes and on the telly. He told me to, I think he said, ask you how was the piccalilli sauce out to Mabel's. He'd seen us together on the other side of his counter, he never forgets an unfriendly face. And how *was* the piccalilli?

—— You really are a bastard.

—— No use being angry with me, John Fist me boy.

St. Dunstan caught me by the nose once with red-hot fire tongs, but look. (Putting a finger on the end of his nose, Breed pushed it to one side, to show that there was no trace of a mark.) Martin Luther threw an inkstand at me once, and another time he drove me away with a fart that was *beyond belief*—but here I be! Oh, son, I have a fun life. Don't get snippety with me.

——— Know any place around where I can buy a long spoon?

John felt the need to protect himself. Getting upset with Breed only made him feel foolish; indeed, he was blushing right now. He pushed himself to say:

——— I'm taking Mona home for the weekend.

——— Splendid! Splendid!

——— You seem to have quite an information-gathering service—you know Mona?

——— Haven't had the pleasure, but I'm sure she's just close enough to right. Right? Your mother will adore her. Right?

John fought back a smile; he really did not want to smile.

Breed said: ——— *Quod Diabolus non potest, mulier efficit.*

——— Spies and Latin. You sound like the goddam British Foreign Office.

——— Peace. You're doing just fine. Want my car?

13

THEY arrived at the house with a glass wall unannounced by letter or phone call. It was early in the afternoon. The front door was locked; John told Mona that his mother was a great one for locking up day and night. Putting their suitcases down (there were two pieces of luggage this time), he ranged on the lawn along the expanse of store-window glass but did not see anyone inside, so he returned to the door and rang the bell.

A long wait; the door opened.

There stood John's mother. Her face began to shimmer, like aurora borealis, with myriad reactions to what she saw. Son. Unknown foreign car. Girl. Suitcases. Son's skiing windbreaker torn at a shoulder seam. One deep look at Mona inhibited her from rushing forward and enfolding her son in her arms. She called out, as if at the sight of fire licking at curtains:

—— Malcolm! Malcolm! My God! Malcolm! Come here!

One of the many notable changes in her expression came while she waited for the succor for which she had thus screamed, as she must suddenly have realized that she, Rowena Fist, who should not even in summer have been caught dead in madras Bermuda shorts, was being surveyed more or less alive in them, in the chill of November, by a pair of liquid brown eyes whose lids had been painted sleepless-night blue.

Now came John's father, contributing his face, so far unshaven that day, to the symphony of reflexes.

Mona was magnificent. Her Bennington aspect had shifted subtly. John reflected in those sweetly time-frozen moments that she looked like a whore trying to look like a college girl trying to look like a whore. She was dressed all in black; her complexion glowed above the turtleneck. Her long dark hair was combed out straight. The principal feature of her costume, drawing John's father's eyes ever down, down, down, was a pair of black patent-leather knee-length boots, of the sort that were vaguely In just then.

From the facial struggles in the doorway, which were like an instant documentary of the Thirty Years' War, dominant themes began to emerge: on his father's visage, marked interest; on his mother's, incredulity.

At last, long after John had muttered an introduction of Mona, his father was able to speak, in a tone half reproachful, half injured, yet entirely official: —— Don't you think you could have let us know you were coming? (Then, in recovery and retreat:) I mean, we're going out

for dinner tonight and lunch tomorrow. We'd like to *see*
you when you come home for a weekend.

—— That's O.K., Dad. We'll find something to do.
Won't we, Mona?

—— Sure, honey.

John's mother was doing some audible breathing, especially on the intake.

During the assignment of a room to Mona and the
settling of suitcases, which followed, John had to be agile
to make sure that no one was left alone with anyone else.
Right at that moment he did not even want a conference
between his mother and father. He became a kind of tour
director for a few moments, herding the whole party
with him wherever he went and singing out observations,
anecdotes, and pleasantries. His parents were still so
stunned that they went along like sheep. It turned out
that John's parents had had lunch; his mother offered to
make sandwiches for the unexpected guests. Mona said
she'd be glad to whip something up, but John's mother
was rather firm on the point of fixing a meal for her son
and her son's date. Date! Mona's voice, perhaps somewhat to John's disappointment, was impeccable. He had
fully expected her to call his mother darling and possibly
sweetie; instead, she put on a deadly-accurate college-girl
mode of speech, with strong whiffs of the Heavenly
Seven, and she was at once respectful and—again with
high fidelity in tonal reproduction—just a tiny bit trucu-
lent, sulky, standoffish.

John's father excused himself and disappeared.

In the kitchen Mrs. Fist picked up all the latest
news.

—— How are things going, son?

—— Fine.

—— How are you enjoying your courses?

—— They're O.K.

—— What do you like best?

—— Duh. I couldn't really say. They're all so-so.

While the children (John loved the idea of his mother thinking of him and Mona as the children) were wordlessly eating, and as his mother washed up the utensils she had used, in sidled Father Fist, rather diffidently, to join the fun. He had shaved, he had put on both a tie and a blue blazer with gun-metal buttons. For what reason? To set an example for the son, who, having removed the torn ski-parka shell, was in a T-shirt? Or for some other reason?

Mona's story was that she went to a junior college called Laidlow, of which Mr. Fist hadn't heard, but, as he modestly said, you couldn't prove anything by that.

—— Mabel, she's our dean, you may be surprised about our calling her by her first name, but she has a completely free attitude, a kind of Summerhill point of view—it's definitely a student-centered place, wouldn't you say, Johnny?

Mona obviously remembered every word the tenure beasts had uttered, and pretty soon, as Malcolm Fist's eyes widened, she began getting into rather meaty educational theories, and she dropped Pestalozzi and Dewey and Kilpatrick and Montessori all over the place. John thought his father was beginning to look plastered. There were unlit half-burned candles in a pair of brass candlesticks on the round breakfast table in the kitchen, and as she conversed with John's father, Mona picked at the drippings and began to roll them between her hands, her warm palms softening the wax. She had eaten quickly all around the insides of her sandwiches, leaving the crusts splayed on her plate for Mrs. Fist to get rid of.

John stood up decisively before he had finished even

his first sandwich and said: —— Come on, Mona, what say we listen to some music?

With an alacrity that made John feel giddy with power, Mona got to her feet, and they left the older generation in the kitchen. John's father looked, indeed, saggingly conscious of his age as John nodded to him on the way out.

During his older brother Siever's high school years, John's father had installed a not-bad hi-fi combination in the living room and had begun buying records, trying to keep abreast of his sons' musical fashion-hopping. John had moved away from rock-'n'-roll to jazz very early; this was one of the things that made him feel "different" at Sheldon. These albums were all old now; John put on three of his post-rock-'n'-roll favorites, Erroll Garner's "Concert by the Sea," Ahmad Jamal at the Pershing, and Brubeck's Storyville album. He and Mona sat on the floor. She pulled off her boots, and he took off his shoes and socks. For a time Mona seemed to drink in the sounds. This was exceedingly pleasant. John felt that the music washed over both of them, hugged them, unified them; at the same time it guaranteed John a safe distance from Mona. He was aware of possibilities of both excitement and danger in intimacy with this bright girl. How she flattered him in the game she was playing!—obeying him, catering to him in front of his father. Could he go through with a real loyalty to her? He was aware of the host of other men who dealt with her; he imagined something like the West Point Corps of Cadets marching along behind her at every moment—so that when he felt combative toward her (as he did when he thought of her leaving those crusts—not a word, not a gesture to his mother of offering to clean up), she seemed formidable, too heavily manned. The thought that there might be

platoons of Emils standing behind her made John tremble
with nausea and outrage. She was sharp and cynical—yet
willing (and able) to give at least an illusion of absolute,
exclusive intimacy with him. Intensely John Fist's very
own unadulterated date.

She now began, however, to be restless. John saw her
gazing into the hexagonal face of a large stone—a
beryl?—set in an old-fashioned ring on the middle finger
of her right hand. Was this some game of image magic?
In the car driving up she had told John, half warning,
half luring, that she was a witch. He had thought, after
she had said that, of Breed; the piece of paper all covered
with fine print. What had those tiny words said?

Rather sharply she had added: —— I said witch, not
bitch.

Now, with her shoulders leaning back against a sofa,
she did indeed look beautifully evil: dark, all in black,
with translucent purple smudges of bad living under her
eyes—some sort of chthonian queen. In a few minutes she
produced from somewhere the drip wax she had taken
from the candle, still malleable, and she began to fashion
a human form—stubby, pyknic, potbellied, gross. She
held it up and said of it, with a look of mischief, con-
spiracy:

—— Your daddy.

A stab of very strange pleasure-and-anger shot
through John. He said:

—— You're some sculptress. That resembles my father about the way the Pietà does my mother. Did you
see it? At the Fair?

—— Listen, honey (she said, ignoring his question),
that blazer of his! How stuffy can you get?

John suddenly wanted the subject thoroughly
changed—why was she so interested in Malcolm Fist?

What right had she to criticize him—to express her interest in him by taking him apart?

Without changing the subject, Mona responded un-
erringly to John's swing, even to the unspoken phrase in
his mind, taking him apart. With the white-enameled nail
of her right little finger she dug into the groin of the little
wax lecher and dug out all that could have been important, and, flicking her finger off her thumb, she skidded
the excision under the sofa.

—— Right, baby?

For some reason John, giving no answer, thought of
Margaret. Of her incredible innocence—and his own.

Some time later he had to go to the bathroom, and
out of an old habit he ran upstairs to his own room, to the
toilet he and Siever had shared. As he sped past his mother's bedroom door on the way there, he heard his mother's
voice; she was on the phone. Afterward, on the way back,
he slowed down passing her door. Perhaps his being in
bare feet had muffled his footsteps so she had not been
aware of his being upstairs. At any rate, he now clearly
heard, over the music downstairs, her words:

—— But, Chloe, there's something funny about her.
That cap on the tooth I mentioned when I called you
before: *It looks like it's made of tin.*

That image, of ultimate cheapness, stayed with John
as he chatted into the late afternoon with Mona; there
was something both unfair and compelling about it. She
was a sharp girl, one who, it could surely be said, lived by
her wits, and her conversation was far more intelligent
than (at random) Wagner's or Gibbon's. She was definitely college material—a dropout in the sense that it
would never have occurred to her to try to get in. She
began talking about, of all things, the cicatrization of the
faces, arms, and thighs of young girls in puberty rites in

Dahomey: something she had picked up, with her astonishing accuracy, from some pipe-smoker. As she was talking of this, John suddenly thought of having sat in the
Freshman Dean's office, one day the year before, and having caught a glimpse of a number beside his name on his
record card on the Dean's desk: 3M242S26. He had seen
the number only a few moments, but it was as if cica-
trized now across his forehead. What was it? Was it a
code for all of his abilities and accomplishments? Or did
it stand for *him*—his data-processed self? His Fist-
machine program? He was now at home; his excited
mother was trembling upstairs for her cub—yet as Mona
spoke of the African ritualist bending over the thighs of
the girl with his special knives, John was overcome with a
horror of the impersonality, the inhumanity of the big
machine of life for which he was being educated. What
good did it do to have a mother? At any moment buttons
might be pressed in that machine that would start a
holocaust and impress his number on a hopeless GI dog
tag; or in some nightmare the number might be projected
with others onto a fantastic heavenly body called Telstar
and be seen, a rubric for a faceless John Fist, all over
Europe, which was part East, part West, or over Africa,
for that matter, which was neither. He didn't like the idea
of being personally caught up in cultural relativity when
it began to be a matter of big numbers. The number 3
was O.K. He, a WASP; Mona, a whore; the African
Negro, a tribal cultist. You could tolerate otherness up to
a point, but somewhere not far beyond three you began
to feel anxiety. John realized, as he inwardly groaned at
the sheer numbers of Africans, that he was becoming intolerant of Mona. One of the three. He picked her because it had become *wrong* to be intolerant of an African.
He began to side with his mother against her. He took

refuge in a certain smugness—a certain cruelty, exclud-
ing Mona from the number of the acceptable. Her gestures. That cap on her tooth. There was indeed something
Not Quite Right about this date.

But Mona had her trade's talents, and one of them
was intuitive quickness. She seemed to see John inside
out, and now she simply settled back and waited for him
to come around to her on one of his circular thoughts.
The music would help her. She hummed—thankfully, for
her waiting game, on pitch. When she finally spoke, John
was restless, ready to go out to her again.

Mona said she could prove she was a witch. She said
she had an extra pair of tits. John laughed nervously.

—— No, really. Supernumerary nipples. To suckle
familiars. It's the oldest and surest test of witchcraft.
What do you think kept those old boys up in Salem going
so long? Looking for *signs* on those young girls' bodies!

She talked on—and John thought he could hear the
echo of a professorial voice resounding in Mona's sentences, which were now both stiff and teasing—about the
authority for this sign, in *Malleus Maleficarum*, of
Kramer and Sprenger, two old boys, Mona said, repeating
that phrase, who helped to put down witches in the fif-
teenth century just by describing them. The vade mecum
of witch-hunters—both Catholic and Protestant—for
hundreds of years.

John thought: Latin from *her*? He began to feel a
pushing up of jealousy. He could barely keep from asking: —— What old boy on our faculty told you that? Was
it good with him?

But now she said: —— Want to see?

Before John could answer she had peeled her
sweater off over her head, and she cupped her hands
under her breasts, which were covered by a white bra,

and leaned her head forward to look down at her torso.

John heard a throat cleared. His father was standing in the living-room doorway.

Malcolm Fist's eyes grew bright as sealed-beam headlights, a blush drowned his features, and he cried out like one who has crashed into someone else because he wasn't watching his step: —— *Excuse* me.

Mona clutched her sweater to her front.

John looked hard at his father's face. There was absolutely nothing there but a rapture of envy.

The father slid backwards around the door jamb and called out from his sightless station in the hall in a cavernous voice: —— Just wondered if you two wanted a cocktail. It's drink time. We have to go out in a bit.

—— Sure, Dad. We'd love one. (Splendid permission! John's voice really filled his throat.)

—— I'll get your mother.

Drinks were awkward, it seemed, for everyone but Mona. John's mother could not keep from staring at her son's bare feet, and John's father obviously tried with all the good will in his heart not to throw agonized looks at Mona's sweater, now of course snugly on again. Mona's intelligence came through, and her tact, and now John felt grateful to her and rather irritable toward both his parents.

They went out. As John and Mona had a second drink together and Mona scrambled some eggs and cooked some bacon (drying the grease from each strip with a paper towel, her fingers flying with delicacy and practice), John felt he wanted her very much. But what was the protocol? She was a guest in his home. Should he offer her money or, in some unclear fashion, seduce her?

Finally, when they were back in the living room, he decided to raise the question openly, and she put a gentle hand on his arm and said: —— Oh, honey, on the house.

Which house? he began to wonder. Then he was hit by a stirring up of qualms. Should there not be more feeling, more real affection than he felt for Mona, in this transaction? He began to think about Margaret in the very moment when he moved his face forward to kiss Mona. His lips fairly skidded on Mona's thick lipstick; her tongue came swiftly forward on professional drill. Remembering Margaret's naïve palm at the back of his neck, he reached for the edge of Mona's sweater, and—

14

In the morning, while John was lathering his face to shave, and just after it crossed his mind that he had been remarkably successful in avoiding a confrontation with either his father or his mother, he heard that throat-clearing again, and then his father's voice:

—— Mind if I come in? I can't seem to get a word with you.

John grunted inhospitably. He felt strongly that the bathroom was man's last castle. How many years had he suffered of being kept out of bathrooms? Just a minute, son; I need a minute's privacy. Was a son not finally entitled to this fort?

His father heard the grunt and was obviously embarrassed, but he plunged into prepared speeches as into a drawn bath—heavily praising Mona, mainly for her brightness.

—— These college kids today. Hell, your mother would never make the grade in competition with a brain like that.

—— Why should Mom (watch that note of alarm!) want to compete with her?

—— I mean people your mother's age and mine wouldn't even have had a look-in with the admissions offices these days, if *we* tried to get in. It's too rugged. I think they're spoiling education.

John scraped at his chin and said nothing.

Then his father asked, in an apologetic voice that suggested he was running an interrogatory errand for Rowena Fist: —— But, ahem, isn't she a little older than you are?

—— I've never asked her. Does it matter?

—— Not now, but later in life. . . .

John wanted to guffaw, but he said: —— I think her seeming older may be an illusion.

—— Illusion?

—— For one thing, she's physically (turn, knife!) very mature for her age.

—— I suppose she is. (As if something of the sort hadn't occurred to Daddy-O!)

—— And then she's been with older people a lot. She knows some of the faculty at Sheldon really quite intimately. . . . But what (what a queer sensation of being a father for a moment!) are you driving at?

At this his father, as if his knees were giving way, tried to sit on the laundry hamper, but the feet of the hamper slid a little on the Evergloss Vinyl Masterbath Tiles, which were guaranteed for a lifetime of eezy kare, and a scramble ensued. John glanced around and saw his father, in suit and tie ready for church, hanging by the elbows on a towel rack; but the son turned back to his shaving as if nothing were happening. Malcolm Fist recovered his balance and stood up.

A counterattack had to follow: —— Look, son, something I've wanted to ask you ever since you arrived yesterday: When did you last see the inside of a barbershop?

Here was a question that lifted John's spirits! Now he was on a rock foundation. John had a sudden feeling of solidarity with the Gutwillig crowd, a consciousness of Lusk, Spinter, Faglio, Breed, as companions with him in a band of intellectual speedsters, a New Type, not-carers for whom the only danger, in matters of appearance, was that idiosyncrasy might become classifiable. His father's generation couldn't get over the conviction that if, even as a student, you were moving toward a certain cluster of careers, you were obliged to wear a certain look. This was all tied in with the ineluctability of the educational conveyor belt now, the relentlessness of the journey from grade school to high school to college to graduate school to military service to a Good Job to a suburb in Megalopolis, where one would beget children and pass on to them the priceless lesson of life: —— Learning equals earning!

—— Oh God, Father, the crew cut went out with the fox trot.

—— That doesn't justify looking like a—like a sick goat doing the—what now?—doing the *frug*? Please get yourself a haircut as soon as you get back tomorrow. Before they boot you out.

By this command, its ultimatum prefaced and compromised by the word please, John's father exposed his most absurd failure of understanding. Malcolm Fist was under the impression that he was Laius, King of Thebes, and that his son John, alias Oedipus, was out for his skin so he could run off with the Queen. But John did not feel that he was living out that cliché myth. He did not think of his father as formidable at all; not as a rival. He regarded Malcolm Fist as a friend, really as a peer. He was a very gentle and decent man who couldn't help saying please. John had warm and relaxed feelings toward him, with a tiny bit of pity mixed in. But his father seemed to have a fixed idea that he should pretend to be stern, strict, an absolute king-figure, in order to give his son something concrete against which to rebel. How out of character! What wild errors echoed on the bathroom walls!

—— Have you chosen (man to boy, leaving the haircut command floating in mid-air) your major for next year?

—— I don't think I'm going to choose one.

—— But you have to, don't you? Or have they dropped *that* now?

John wondered if he had been furious with Spinter, when Spinter had ranted against the major, precisely because Spinter had been so right.

—— Any man who is a man (John said) has to be able to move in any direction he wants to. Or not move.

As John uttered that slogan—yes, he admitted to himself, it might qualify for the game of Slogans—his father's face appeared in the mirror over his shoulder, and it was so solemn, so torn, so tired, so baffled, that John felt a sudden stab of self-doubt that was actually physically painful. The Mona joke wasn't funny after all. Maybe John, not his father, was the absurd one. That shot face in the mirror was the face of a decent man who had tried his best but was caught like every other Ameri-

can man in the vise between principles and slogans, between a set of so-called values of a strict and puritan cast
and a set of guidelines for getting away with as much as
one could in everyday life. What had brought his father's
disappointment if not the very slogan John had just
mouthed?

John suddenly thought of Grandpa Newson, standing on his hands on the dock of the Club de Oficiales at
Matanzas—how powerful he had been, though small of
stature! Sure of himself and of all else in relation to himself. Mum had taken after him and so couldn't have mar-
ried a man as powerful as he—or as she. No, Malcolm
Fist was no king; he had always let Siever and Lisa and
John go about their affairs in their own various ways—
until, now, John really thought himself wiser than his
father. Nor had his father tried to cover up his unkingli-
ness by insisting on a lot of phony obeisances and silences
and even obediences. And indeed now, in the privacy the
two of them shared in a bathroom, John realized, as he
washed the last of the lather from his face, that his father
had never shouldered him with any part of the load of a
father's defeat.

——Excuse me, Pop (he said, going into his bedroom to dress, leaving the old man staring at himself in
the mirror).

15

JOHN's mother was waiting for him at the breakfast table. She, too, was dressed for church and had even already put on a hat. John could not help feeling that she had dressed partly for him—she was in a pale-blue suit with a white piqué ruff at the neck and white piping all down the lapels and at the cuffs; an outfit a bit too virginal for her. As he approached the table he gave her a long penetrating look, trying to see her as his father must see her—trying to account for his father's persistent furtive peeking at Mona. Was Jocasta no longer desirable? She must have been fine-looking when she had been young—nutbrown hair, a straight small nose, high blush of the Scottish side and infinity-blue eyes of the Lowlands side, and an economical body that must have been packed with driving cross-court shots and wild plunges into the surf and spirited arguments late at night—all tuned tight and vibrant like a harp; a light knock on the curved neck of this beautiful instrument must have shaken all the wrest pins, and out must have come a hum of all the tones and overtones. But now? John felt as if he had plucked his father's haunted eyes off that steamy bathroom mirror and brought them along with him. John thought of what had happened on the living-room floor the night before, and looked at this mother with his own eyes and his father's eyes, and shuddered, and sat down.

As was her way, she started right in: —— Mona's precious.

What a queer, loaded word!

John said: —— Don't you know I can't start thinking until I have some fuel in the furnace? (This was from his mother's old line, repeated on a thousand mornings, trying to persuade him to eat a big breakfast before going to school.)

—— Didn't you bring any decent clothes? Aren't you and Mona going to church with us?

—— You mean (a cruel impulse) I should make an honest woman of her?

—— No, I only meant—

—— Good God, Mother, we're off on a weekend, Mona'll probably sleep right through lunch.

John happened to look at his mother's face and saw that she was suddenly close to tears. She blurted out:

—— What turned you into a beatnik?

—— Beatnik? I despise beatniks. (Very calm voice.) You're miles out of touch. Beatniks went out five years ago: the fourteen-year-olds have taken it up now. You haven't the faintest idea what a beatnik was.

—— Those bare feet.

—— In my own house?

—— Propped up on the coffee table. If you could see the bottoms of them.

—— Shoes get dirty, too. Mother, beatniks were never serious; the whole thing was sterile. Where have you *been*? What do you think I *am*?

Mrs. Fist's face was too hot now for tears, as she said: —— You have no . . . Sleeping around in motels! I've *heard* about the college girls and their pessaries and emotions don't enter into it . . .

John realized all at once his strength, and during a long pause, sipping at his orange juice, he put on a rather mysterious air: but this collapsed as he thought of his childish innocuousness in the motel room with Margaret; he could not help breaking out a belchlike laugh. This drove him to a swift change of tactics:

—— It was you who read *Peyton Place* around here, not me. *The Carpetbaggers!* You accuse *me* of sleazy—

—— I didn't accuse you of anything. I just asked a perfectly reasonable question—if you were going to church on a Sunday morning.

—— Listen, Mom . . .

—— Don't *call* me that. (And John saw all too clearly in her face the horror she felt at all the standardized notions that the word Mom evoked: sexual frigidity, rejection of her children, a methodical grinding down of her husband.)

—— My God, I always have since I was two. Either that or Mum.

—— I don't care. Don't call me that.

She had provided the opening and he moved in in full panoply.

—— All right, since we've covered the topic of my

feet, why don't we get onto the question of *you* for **a** minute?

Mrs. Fist sat up a little straighter.

—— You can sound off about those pessaries—I remember when that case came up in Walboro, the fifteen-year-old girl who got mixed up in unusual practices with a dozen businessmen, pillars all—how you talked about the moral infantilism of American men! You always expected Siever and me—the men!—to be hard on ourselves, self-control, self-discipline—you never would let me stroke Ptolemy in back of his rib cage, said it was *disgusting;* did you ever watch yourself lick the butter off your fingers when you finished a roll? Always trying to push good clean-cut American health down our throats. Vitamin pills: I remember the aftertastes. Vi-Penta. Unicaps. God, there was even cod-liver oil for a while there. And you? I've seen the way you nibble at those little chocolate-covered after-dinner mints, only you eat them after breakfast: Did you think their being called Thins would make you that way? And look at the makeup for church! You talk about Our Heritage, about old things being the best things—but now you're terrified of getting old yourself. Mom is bad enough, but Grandma! Is *that* why you're so puckered up about me bringing a girl home?

As John reached this peak of vindictiveness, he was hit very hard by a wave of astonishment, sympathy, grudging love for his mother. Why in God's name was he saying such things? He had seen her, as he poured out this random venom, lean forward with something like real interest on her face. Far from cringing, she seemed to be flowering. How he admired her guts! And yet he could not stop:

—— Dad can't even begin a story when there are

guests around without you getting up and offering people
the hors d'oeuvres and making like a hostess till the whole
thread, point, of his story is lost—if there was a point.
Everybody gets the picture: He's a great big bore.

Now John's mother looked positively glowing—as if
John's tirade had led to one simple conclusion: Malcolm
Fist is a bore. She stood up and smoothed down the pale-
blue fabric at her hips.

—— You're behaving (she said) the way you did six-
seven years ago. So *aggressive*. And your hunger, you eat
like a jackal or a buzzard or something, it's sick-making. I
taught you to be a clean boy. Look at your room, you
haven't been here twenty-four hours and just look at it.

John wondered what they were really squabbling
about. His bringing a woman home? The passage of
years? The struggle between creativity and decomposition
in his once wonderful mother? Her despair that she
wasn't making anything, shaping anything, any more?

But where were these pains? A rosy look of warmth
and generosity was spreading on her face, and she said:

—— Is this girl you brought home really the one you
wrote us about?

—— No, it isn't really.

John had answered without thinking, without being
able to think. And then, realizing what he had admitted,
and what his mother had understood, he was suddenly in
a passion of anger at her, incomparably more searing
than the mere petulance he had felt a minute before.

He stood up and stalked out of the dining room, and
he ran upstairs and burst into Lisa's room, where Mona
was sleeping with the blankets pulled right up over her
head, and he shook her shoulder and pulled the covers
down to let the light in. What a wrinkled bag she was in
the refuge of sleep! She groaned and stirred.

He said: —— Come on. Get up. I have to go back.

And as soon as she was ready they left, just walked out and drove off. John didn't give as much as a goodbye to either parent. Mona was sulky, and kept saying:

—— Coffee, give me coffee.

16

SURELY this was it. The sense of melting, of gliding into a warm presence—fusion. There had been an impression of a garden, a maze of boxwood and then the measured green rooms of an orchard, and weeds, and a young girl climbing apple limbs; blue cotton cloth, the gold of her thighs. Then he was stepping through filtered sunlight toward a dim shape of marvelous sensuality, womanness; feminine hands were raised, offering him something, and then an embrace in which he seemed to press into and through the other—fusion. Would he come? The sensation of warmth, of floating! . . .

He wakened.

His heart wrenched at its moorings and suddenly

began to run. He thought for a moment, as he rode the tachycardia with frigid hands and feet, that he was going to die.

He realized how cold he was. Most of his covers had slid off the bed, the air in the room was bitter, Flack had thrown the windows wide open. But he could not cover himself. He seemed paralyzed by a terrifying sense of loss, for he had been cheated, horribly cheated: the wonderful warmth had only been dream stuff. Breed! Breed had cheated him—had promised and welshed. Where had the empty weeks gone? Time, like the night air and John's arms, was frozen, his heart raced and yet time was stuck. Was this death? Was death an eternity of a senselessly pounding heart and an inability to move?

Now John's mind began to work at fragments of this frozen hell. This was winter. This was the deep hole of midwinter. The Christmas vacation had been a disaster. More recently: Spinter's challenge, Margaret's reproachful letter, Breed's increasing mockery, Mona forgotten and not forgotten. A great deal of reading, as if working hard; but going to no classes. A floater in non-time. From home—silence. The longest silence he had ever known from home.

Gradually, gradually, as he visited these corners of reality, his plunging heart slowed down. Cold as he was, he found himself covered with sweat. He managed at last to rise and with chattering teeth he went and closed the bedroom window; he lifted his covers from the floor and as though casting a net threw them outspread on the bed, and then got in among the thoughts that were caught there.

Now he was irretrievably far from sleep, and he began to range backwards and forwards in the darkness.

Christmas. He had wanted, as he had put it to him-

self, to get shut of sentimentality. He had actively not
wanted the nostalgic excitement of going downstairs in
his own home on the morning of baby Jesus' birthday and
seeing the pile of bright-papered presents under the tree,
his mother wanting him to unwrap things in a certain
definite order; so he had suggested to Breed that they get
Margaret and some other volunteer cheese and go up skiing, take part of a house, keep house for themselves. But
Breed said he wouldn't go to Vermont for fear of being
put in a pie by those people up there and being baked.
Breed's lousy devil-jokes. All of which seemed to turn out
to have meaning—for John had gone up alone, and he
might as well have been put under crust and shoved in
the oven. The snow had been crummy; the group of
young marrieds in his boarding house had been soused
the whole time, one long soak, and the gents had been
given to close harmony, too close—they diminished the
thirds too far, till the intervals were inhuman: off-pitch
electronic music from larynxes of flesh. And he had run
out of money. He had tried to borrow from some of the
drunks and had been brutally snubbed, and had wired his
father, and—paradoxical disappointment, even humilia-
tion—his father had sent too much money within a matter of hours, with a telegram: WE ARE GLAD TO KNOW
WHERE YOU ARE. He had felt Breed's bargain hanging over
him the whole time: *when would he feel the first breakthrough?*

After the vacation, one night, Breed had pumped the
whole Mona joke out of him.

Breed, when the story was all told: —— Know who
the real witch is?

—— Who?

—— Not Mona. The essence of witchery is *male-
ficium.*

125

—— I suppose you mean my mother.

—— The essence of the thing is what a witch *does*—her power to inflict damage. She sends blight on your tomatoes. Your house cat comes down with distemper—she sends it. Snow on your TV screen—she's throwing dust in your eyes. Your house catches fire, a front tire blows out. Parkinson's disease. Schizophrenia. Coronary occlusion—oblivion.

—— You mean (affecting an airy tone to offset a nibbling of fear) dear old Mum can do all that?

Breed had merely grinned. And now, warmed somewhat by the blankets, John was pierced by regret for the dream-warmth of which he had been cheated. He wanted —he realized he had been wanting for weeks—to punish his mother (why not Breed?) for cheating him. But now he saw that it hadn't been enough simply to cut the cord of communication; it wasn't enough just not to show up, not to write to her, not to speak to her. She was too strong; she had gone silent. Who was punishing whom?

Then he thought of something he could do: he could drop out.

But he rejected that at once. That would hurt his father more than her. The idea of leaving Sheldon made him think again of Spinter (did thinking of his father, he wondered, make him think of Spinter?), and of a session just a couple of nights before, during which, as Spinter sounded off, John became fascinated watching himself listen—for he saw himself grow furious with Spinter, but in the very middle of his fury he seemed to realize that in a few days this anger might modulate again, move off Spinter, be aimed at others including, in the end, himself, as he came round to subscribing to Spinter's originally hateful views. They'd been talking about Selma, and Martin Luther King's kind of love, and through mention of Andy Goodman and Mike Schwerner the role of Jews in the Negro revolution had come into it: at first Spinter had seemed to direct his shafts mainly at Faglio and only secondarily at John:

—— The reason some Negroes are anti-Semitic is that they can't stir Jews up with accusation the way they can you Christians or ex-Christians, whatever you are. Jews can't work up a real sweat of guilt for the crimes of slavery, the way you can. All that time when you Puritans —Catholics and Calvinists, Dom, you were all Puritans— were using the Negroes as a bunch of dogbodies, the Jews were just scraping along with their own old familiar troubles, mostly in Europe. They weren't slave-owners, the word ghetto was their word. Nowadays in political action the Negroes' big leverage is guilt, and they just can't get the Jews off the ground in the guilt department, because the Jews don't feel it. This is very galling.

Faglio, pale as milk: —— What about all that buying up, after Reconstruction? The early Du Bois books are full of it.

Spinter, deftly shifting gears (and now John felt the sharp gaze on himself): —— The trouble with you Christians, or ex-Christians, is, you still believe in Hell but you don't believe in Heaven any more. (John felt suddenly alert: Was Breed somehow hiding in that sentence?) You've given up *trying*. Look. We've got our big drive all set for next week on this majoring business, we're really going to let her rip—and how many WASPs do you think we can get to go along? I don't know, like *three*. What the hell's the matter with you, Fist? You're not making use of your days the way a good Calvinist should. You don't think about them harps and wings the way you ought to.

John had felt the fury then, and he had blushed and

been unable to speak. He had wanted to say that he thought the idea of picketing the Dean's office on the subject of majoring was one of the screwiest and most naïve ideas he'd ever heard of. What did they expect to accomplish that way? Weren't they playing games, playing at Gutwillig's charades—playing union, playing underdog, playing Negro? Why not just come right out and carry placards with obscenities on them, like those characters out at Berkeley? That had more point than this crappy agitation about majoring. But he had just turned aside and said nothing. . . .

That bull's eye over the "i" had made him open the letter right in front of his mailbox. A silly letter, only a few petulant sentences—but how Margaret's words had stayed with him! She had waited and waited. He had promised to call. (He hadn't.) She didn't think he was all that callus.

He had said nothing to Spinter and he had done nothing about Margaret, apart from overcoming a mild temptation to send the letter back with the spelling corrected.

Whenever he thought of going out to see Mona, to take Mona and talk with Mona, he thought of her face when he had yanked those covers down and exposed her to the light, on that Sunday morning, just before church time, up home. How Breed had laughed at John's rueful description of that unveiling! Breed's mockery had become more and more succinct. Now all he needed to do was to let a facial muscle pull, curve an eyebrow, and John felt the sting.

17

AT a little before eleven that morning, John found himself in a dark hallway in Humblesmith, standing in his wet raincoat outside a single-leafed swinging door which had, at face level, a small oval glass window to help prevent collisions. Through this oval John looked downward into the bowl of a lecture amphitheater, smelling dried linseed oil on the wood of the door as he leaned close against it. On the stage stood old man Orreman, flushed with the delights of peroration, his white hair a nimbus of inspiration around his craggy head, his arms raised as if he were obliged to hold off the ground the whole weight of his argument for the past hour, his face joyful over the labor, his eyes huge and gleaming. Through the door his words came only as a series of sonorous, passionate vowels, so that to John, in the end, the old man's deep feelings were simply absurd:

—— Oo uh ooo i ooo ah o o . . .

The mouth closed; the arms fell; the face went dark like a suddenly turned-off light bulb. Long before the last echo of the last vowel died, or would have if it hadn't been drowned out, the students were jostling each other up the aisles toward John. Quickly he pushed his way inside, met the shock of the oncoming haste, and, caroming from shoulder to shoulder, forced his way down against the flow.

Orreman was squaring his papers on the podium.

—— Sir?

The big eyes moved to John and, devoid of recognition, held on him.

—— Could I see you a minute, sir?

The professor lifted his papers, reached behind him for his ancient briefcase, which lay waiting on a chair, stuffed the papers in it, fastidiously clasped the worn strapping, and then lurched with his up-and-down stride across the small stage toward the steps to the floor level where John stood. John felt like a horse being approached by a hostler holding a halter. Yes, the old teacher gripped his arm, steered him toward a door beside the stage, and said:

—— Lead me to my office. Room 113.

Oval Ears' whole office reminded John of the glimpse he had had that other morning of the inside of the old man's briefcase. This was a challenge not for a janitor but for an archaeologist: Asturian kitchen middens? Schleswig-Holstein reindeer-hunters' Mesolithic rubble? Maglemosian culture of Yorkshire—burins, microliths, and all? It was incredible. How did the old man keep track of his lecture notes? There were a decrepit leather-covered sofa, a desk chair, and an ancient Morris chair with its footrest extended, but all these perches were so heaped with intellectual detritus that the entire interview had to be conducted on the hoof.

—— The name again?

—— Fist. John Fist. Son of Malcolm Fist.

Orreman's magnified eyes aimed themselves at John, and John could not for his life read them. Surprise? Rebuke? The old man's trembling hand reached into the inside breast pocket of his hairy black suit coat, and it drew forth a long, narrow, flexible-covered notebook. He opened it. A forefinger ran down a column at the left, then stopped.

—— Ah yes, I see. You're deficient, young fellow. You owe me two papers. You've let this become very serious.

—— That's what I came to talk with you about, sir. (John felt that he was saying sir too often; he hated the word.) I've lost interest.

Now the eyes were legible. Incredulity. How could a student not be interested, let's say, in Sylvian Orreman's lecture on the abolition of the mortgaging of one's own person, under Solon?

—— I wanted to tell you, sir, I'm thinking of leaving Sheldon.

The old man was suddenly mobilized: —— And you want me to tell you not to . . . not to quit. Is that it? I can't help you, Mr. Fist. That was a first-rate paper you did on your Myrmidon play at Dionysia, but I can't help you. There's nothing in my whole stock (the old man grandly waved his arm to indicate the riches of ancient times in these shambles on desk, chairs, floor)—nothing to deal with just lying down on the job.

John exploded: —— First-rate? God, sir, you gave me a D on that paper.

—— That was to encourage you.

—— Sir, I feel like one of us is off his rocker.

—— Not at all. Just out of reach of each other. Maybe we could try the telephone—maybe if there were in fact some distance between us. . . . Your father—did you tell me one day that he's now . . . ?

—— Yes, sir. Fake antiques.

—— I thought that was what you said. I don't suppose you know what you're going to do? The usual cattle boat?

—— You were the one person I didn't think would put me in a slot, in a category. Like, he's the cattle-boat type. Anyway, cattle boats are out, now. Nobody does that any more. They've been out three or four years. Where have you been, sir?

—— I'm sorry, Mr. Fist. I . . . I don't know you young men any more.

—— That's pretty obvious.

—— Not that I haven't spent a great deal of painful thought on you. (John had worked himself between Orreman and the light, and now all he saw on the thick glasses were reflections of the high window, with a pair of small, dark silhouettes of himself bisecting the two glistening shapes.) I've struggled to keep up. The closest I can come to a suggestion is this: I think your best bet lies with following someone like Epictetus. You boys fancy yourselves as Diogenean—barefoot friars who despise so-called good things, and for whom the essence of virtue is independence—but cynic means dog-like, Fist, cynicism really comes down to snarling, when it's vulgarized the way you campus philosophers do vulgarize everything. And part of the time you seem to think Epicurus has it for you—cut out all learning that doesn't do anything for you; simple pleasures; freedom from fear, especially from fear of Hell. (John moved a step away.) But I really believe that what you need is a little less parietal freedom and a little more stoicism. There's a good deal of cynicism in real stoicism, you know: All real things are material, even the soul, which is a sort of atomic gas, and when we die all that disappears. The balloon simply deflates, either with a bang or with a slow leak. The sage, then, should be dispassionate, he should not be pushed around by pleasure or pain, but he should accede to natural laws—those are laws you just can't break. Nor can you change them with all the sitdowns and placard-carrying in this world.

The old man, in the very moment of saying that a wise man should not be swayed by passion, was evidently deeply so, and John, touched, persuaded, and horrified, began to edge toward the door. Orreman, too, seemed to feel that the interview was over, and he said:

—— My dear Mr. Fist (putting a hand on the knob of the office door), failure doesn't consist in negative judgments from without. It comes from within—a drying up, a diminution of response. . . . Why don't you try coming back to class? (God, the old faker *had* been aware of his absence!) I enjoy lecturing to men like you, John—to troubled sons of men I remember as having been quite untroubled. Of course my memory is going. . . .

The door was wide open.

On the way back to his room John realized how envious he had been, while standing at that oval porthole in the door at the top of the hall, envious of the other students in the amphitheater. Not because they were hearing, as he was not, what the shallow old fart was saying, but for some other reason he couldn't get straight in his mind. He toyed with the idea of going to some of his classes again to find out what this was. To classes other than old Oval Ears', that was for sure.

18

Down the center of Planique Street came the first surge of the demonstration—a clot of students, some carrying placards, many shouting and cursing, faces twisted with anger at what they saw ahead of them: a roadblock of town cops.

Six motorcycle policemen were sitting on their machines, abreast, closing the throat of the street at the crossing with Fourth. A patrol wagon, with several officers standing around it, was parked at the far side of the intersection.

John was on the scene quite by chance; he had been to Breed's room, vaguely looking for a quarrel, but he had found the room empty, and just now, on his way back to his own building, had walked out through the arch from the Forrestal Complex and was standing at the curb, for some reason vividly conscious of the dirty stone of the heavy nineteenth-century buildings behind him.

It was Saturday morning, and John saw that there were quite a few girls in the mob. They were weekend dates—activist types. The month was March, the temperature was in the low fifties, there were dingy heaps of plowed snow melting in the gutters, yet one of the girls at the front of the crowd had bare feet; she was evidently in dead earnest about life, a woman of firmest principles.

Spinter was leading them all; he looked gaunt, with great pools of foul March weather in the hollows under his eyes. He was carrying a crudely hand-printed cardboard placard:

ABOLISH THE MAJOR:
INTELLECTUAL IRON MAIDEN

Back where the crowd was about three deep John saw the tall figure of Professor Gutwillig, who appeared to be furious at having been jostled from a place of leadership into such an unprominent position. He was making swimming motions with his hands and arms, trying to break through to the front, but if he was moving at all in the mob, it was only to lose yet more ground.

The motorcycle cops, like watchdogs growling, were revving their motors: *voom, voom, r-r-r-umm.*

There was little Faglio near the front. What struck John at once was that his face looked exactly like Spinter's. These two had disagreed on every important issue in every discussion John had heard them have, yet now their emotions appeared to be identical: sensuously grim, furious at all authority. Each time a motorcycle rumbled, it was as if the shadows of identical hawks' wings crossed their cheeks.

The front of the crowd was now about fifty feet from

the policemen, and it began to slow down. Even the most dedicated leaders, unsure of the cops' intentions, no doubt already rehearsing on their lips the phrase police brutality, had begun to hang back.

Now a student wearing a dirty quilted olive-green windbreaker jumped forward from the leading edge, turned to face the mob, and, walking backwards, raised his arms and shouted, as if to remind:

—— Non-violent! Non-violent!

His cries, so far as they were heard over the chatter of the crowd and the snarling of the motors, were greeted by what sounded to John like boos, laughter, and admonitions to cut the crap. John wondered if he could be hearing right.

For a moment, as the gap between the crowd and the line of cops narrowed to just a few feet, gaunt Spinter seemed full of a dreadful vitality, which John could not help admiring in a detached way. Spinter's arms were chopping the air with the placard, as if he could unmount and unman the fiercest of cops with its cardboard edge. How excited Spinter really was! And how cut off from that excitement John felt: To him, Spinter was, at that moment, a kind of marvel, like the puny tailor in the fable who slew seven with one blow. At the same time John thought that he despised Spinter's obsession, his single-minded wild stare.

Then John felt a lick of envy much like the one he had experienced the other day peeking into the Humble-smith amphitheater. How had he become such an outsider? He had thought he had nothing but contempt for the demonstrators, yet now he found himself yearning to be in the thick of their cause.

At this strong pull toward the angry-looking joy of the marchers, John thought of something Breed had quoted from a book of Aldous Huxley's, about crowd delirium: how merely being in a multitude delivers a man from his sense of self, so that he slides down into an almost subhuman role, free of all responsibility, conscience, even discrimination—lost in the common thrill, feeling a glow of virtue in the collective crowd-drunkenness, really on the shoulder of a cloud like that provided by a truth drug or light hypnosis; and how easy the further downward slide is, then, into violence.

Immobilized by these eddying thoughts, John remained on the curb, watching.

He heard the barefoot girl shout some long metallic sound at the cops, but he could not make out what it meant. While her mouth remained open a vein on her forehead and one on her neck became inflated, as if she were air-filled and were being squeezed, a shrill bagpipe going into battle.

John looked at the row of faces of the policemen, under their glistening white motorcyclists' helmets. Their jaws were set under their fleshy cheeks, like so many miniature bulldozer blades, in an absolute lock of town-and-gown hatred, which was soundly based on many years of their having grown up in Sheldon Township resenting the carelessly snobbish college boys; yet John also thought he saw fear there—surely not so much fear of action as fear of intellection, a fear, perhaps, that these students, who had had dazzling privileges, might start lecturing them right there in the street on economics, social justice, metaphysical poetry, quantum theory. The front wheels of their motorcycles were uniformly turned sharp left, probably in some sort of readiness for rapid dismounting, but it looked to John as if they might all turn and bolt if the students began throwing brickbats of knowledge at them.

Consternation, however, in the avant-garde. The front ranks, while conscious of leadership, were conscious also of leaning back against the pushing crowd behind. While still cutting down paper enemies with his cardboard halberd, Spinter had braced his feet and was using his shoulder blades to try to hold back his army. The accordion was closing. Those behind were inexorably moving up. The non-violent partisan was violently shaking his fists to heaven and screaming for a halt, which was not forthcoming. Some distance back Professor Gutwillig had his hand raised, as if he wanted to recite, wanted to be heard by the Teacher of Riots, whoever he might be.

The cops, all at once, stepped off their machines; each held a billybat.

Then John saw a flash of khaki: skinny, long-haired Lusk, the graduate student who peddled mimeographed lectures, underdressed in the raw air as usual, rushed forward and pushed at the tanklike chest of one of the cops. By the force of his shove against the immovable man, Lusk propelled himself like a shot, arms and legs flying, backward toward the crowd. But that little rush began it. The gap closed. There began to be a mixing up; shouts, grunting, clubs flicking overhead.

John, sweeping his eyes back over the now tight-packed disorder, met, quite close at hand, the gaze of Chum Breed, which now seemed to John to have been on him all along. Of course it had. Breed's frozen face suddenly broke into a grin; he waved to John—beckoned.

Almost involuntarily John stepped down from the curb and into the mob, and he made his way to Breed's side.

Breed hissed in his ear: —— See how cheerful everyone is!

Suddenly everything changed for John. He no longer saw a clash of abstract forces; he was in a rather quiet eddy of a human stream, where no one seemed to know exactly, or care much, what was happening. True, gloomy reports were being handed down by a beacon of a man, a basketball freak more than seven feet tall whom John had met once, a student named Plark who was the recipient of a scholarship for the simple reason that he might never stop growing and could already stuff, rather than toss, the basketball into the ring; his head was supported far, far above the crowd on a neck that had to be seen to be believed, in which, when he spoke, an Adam's apple struggled hopelessly like a little rabbit just swallowed alive by a boa constrictor.

—— Unk! (he said, presumably responding to the downbeat of a policeman's club on a student's head). That was bad. Oh, man! They've got one of the Murphys' helmets! They're throwing it in the air!

But no one was paying attention to Plark. One student next to John was saying to his neighbor:

—— Have you read *The Rector of Justin?*

—— You mean you read for fun?

—— Good God, no, we had to read it for Pol Sci 77. Picture of power elite. Forward thrust of nineteenth century.

—— No, but I had to read *Herzog*.

—— How come?

—— It was assigned in Totems and Scrotums.

—— Come again?

—— Religion and Sexuality 102. It's Cranston's course. Really great.

To John's other side a student and his date had their arms around each other and were hugged tight together, kissing hard. Then the boy lowered his head, parted her long straight hair at the side with his nose, and began to nibble at her ear. Beside the lovers stood a thin, earnest-looking boy holding a placard:

ELIMINATE FRENCH 27
FIRE PROFESSOR JEJUNE
Every Lecture a Double-Strength Nembutal Capsule

The lover, having sated himself at the earlobe, suddenly raised his face to this boy and, while stroking his date's canvas-covered bottom with both hands, said:

—— I had Jejune last year. What a bomb.

—— We think we've got him (the sign-bearer said). Nineteen of us have agreed to flunk his course to show the Administration how stupid he is.

Breed nudged John and pointed across the crowd.

Sighting along Breed's forefinger, John saw, about twenty feet away, Margaret's face. The crowd near her was becoming turbulent, and she was being bumped here and there, but her face was serene, accepting, as innocent as ever. John left Breed and began to try to force his way through the press toward her, but near her the mob had become especially congested; he was aware of white helmets nearby. He made little progress. He saw that Margaret was with the two students with whom she had been standing when he had seen her for the first time in front of the Co-op that day. He raised an arm and waved it, wanting to catch her eye, but so much was going on that this motion meant nothing. Out of the corner of his eye John became conscious of a white crash hat quite close at hand. The students nearby were having a very good time. John was no longer particularly interested in getting to Margaret, yet he kept trying. What would be the point of reaching her? What was the point of anything? John felt, in the midst of the shouting, the laughter, the cries of pain and anger, that none of this was really happening; it was all somehow an invention, a contrivance, of Breed's. He saw Professor Gutwillig grab Margaret from behind; the intellectual rocket of the Political Science Department crossed his arms in front of Margaret and put a hand on each of her breasts and pressed close against her, while at the same time his face looked full of protest and his mouth seemed to be shouting Slogans. John cared less than ever about what was happening, about anything, yet for some reason he tried with renewed energy to get through to Margaret.

Then he was conscious of a shouting red face, capped with enameled white, right in front of his own. A gilt number shining on the white crown caught his eye: 13. Looking back at the face, John half expected, without caring, to see Breed's features there. But no, the face of a middle-aged stranger, streaming sweat in clammy March. Grimaces. Shouts. John felt a kind of heaviness; was barely interested. He looked at the purple lips and saw, rather than heard, some of the words:

—— It's nothing to you. You smart little prick. Think you're so unblemished. (At that extraordinary choice of a word, John's attention momentarily stirred, but at once drained off.) Come on. Stand up and defend yourself.

John realized that it was precisely his indifference that had insulted and enraged the policeman, but he could not rouse himself to answer, and the cop's fury was redoubled. The angrier the cop grew, the more bored John became—and vice versa.

With a roar the cop pounced at John, grasped him by the shoulders, and began backing out of the crowd, pulling John after him. They made rapid progress that way and soon broke out into the open. Taking John by an upper arm, much as Professor Orreman once had done, the cop led him to the paddy wagon. Half an hour later John Fist was in jail.

19

THE college band was split right down the middle on whether to take part in the Welcome Back Parade for the Seventeen. The seventeen, that is, who had been arrested during the demonstration. In the end four trumpets, one trombone, six clarinets, a saxophone, two piccolos, one snare drum, and the glockenspiel turned out; the music they made as the procession rounded into Planique Street was wholly without foundation, because among others the bass drum and the entire tuba section had decided to disagree, stay away. John, walking among the campus heroes at the head of the line, idly wondered if there was any significance in this. Did men who chose instruments of the lower registers tend to be conservative? Phlegmatic, and therefore unresponsive to hysteria? Or just lazy?

According to the Sheldon *College Courier*, a copy of which had somehow been sneaked into the town lockup that morning, the Sheldon Student Rights Forum had, right after the demonstration, put on a drive entitled Crash for Cash—Go for Dough—Bail the Jail; and within seventeen hours and ten minutes of the last arrest, the Forum's student chairman, Tendon Brown, who was furious at not having been roped in himself, plunked seventeen times sixty dollars down on the police desk at Town Hall.

The streets were lined with students, faculty, and townspeople. Although there was a smattering of clapping and some scattered hissing, John thought that the spectators were mostly just like him—completely unimpressed, puzzled, fogbound.

Near the corner of Planique and Elm, where the onlookers were somewhat more crowded and demonstrative, a man suddenly burst from the sidewalk and rushed out to shake hands with the heroes, one by one. He walked backwards as the heroes advanced. It was Professor Gutwillig, looking peevish in his congratulatory ecstasy.

He took John's hand in both of his and pumped it hard. John observed that Professor Gutwillig was very good at walking backwards; this genius could do anything, and do it well.

—— Nice going, Fist. You've clinched an A with me. I didn't think you were going to *move* this term. Splendid splendid splendid.

The professor sidestepped, while backtracking, and moved on to the next hero. John noticed that Professor Gutwillig knew the name of each of the students who had been arrested.

John himself was in a bad humor. He had slept poorly on the lockup floor the night before; a group of half a dozen of his jailmates, including Spinter and Lusk, had sat up in one corner of the room until very late, singing "We Shall Overcome."

John wanted out. Why couldn't he simply step over to the sidewalk and extricate himself from this incredible snarl of irony, absurdity, and mistaken identity? John Fist a campus hero for his part in the majors demonstration? At one point he actually tried to turn aside, but he found he could not. He was really a Gutwillig boy now—was that it? A for Lack of Effort. Marching along with Spinter and Lusk.

In the midst of these thoughts he spotted Breed in the crowd on the sidewalk. When John first noticed it, Breed's face had that Ice Age look John had seen at first out in the demonstration the day before, but as soon as their eyes met, now, one of Breed's eyelids began to droop, and the face melted around a broad, mischievous, evil wink.

Left, right, left, right. The bottomless band was playing a Freedom Song. All of John's feelings were now focused around that wink of Breed's. What a cheat his contract had so far proved to be! Where were the soaring ecstasies Breed had promised, where even were the acts of nihilism, deviltry, destructiveness? John felt that, far from shooting back and forth to the sharpest extremes of experience, he was, rather, drifting sluggishly through life, like a waterlogged log. He had lost the sense of control over his existence without gaining anything in its place. He remembered, thinking of the wink, what Wagner had said once about Breed: *He drags a guy down.*

The procession halted in front of the Painter Complex. Spinter climbed on top of a car that was parked at

the curb, faced the marchers, raised his arms, and pro-
nounced a kind of benediction of protest:

—— . . . We won't give an inch. . . . We've got a real
great cause. . . . We'll back 'em off the map. . . .

As Slogans, John thought, these of Spinter's were dis-
tinctly thin, prosaic, flat. World-shy Margaret did better
—that one about the lifeboats, men first, women second,
children last. Did leaders of action have to have tin ears?
Then for an unbelievable moment, John had a fantasy of
standing himself on the hardtop, addressing the crowd
with heartbreaking eloquence. . . . *Watch it, now! Are
you going to take yourself seriously as a hero? Why didn't
you drop out of the march? That wink of Breed's!*

Then the crowd broke up, and John went to his
room.

On his doorplate was a note:

*John Fist. You have an appointment with Dean
Littlegas at 2 p.m. on Monday, March 15. Do not
fail to keep.*

That would be the afternoon of the next day.

20

JOHN sat up all night reading *Victory* (Breed stayed away), and by two the next afternoon he was lead-lidded. He went to the Dean's office on time and was ushered right in.

John had not seen the inside of the Dean's office before. Dean Littlegas was obviously a railroad nut. The walls were covered with prints of famous locomotives, and on tables there were four models of engines in glass cases the size of balanced aquariums. Seeing John's sleepy eyes on these exhibits, the Dean got up from behind his desk and moved from model to model, seeming in John's imagination to be wearing an engineer's hat made of mattress ticking.

—— Interested in these? This is Old Ninety-six of the
D. L. and W.; what we used to call the Delay, Linger,
and Wait. (Then, in a tone of disappointment at John's
failure to respond:) Delaware, Lackawanna, and Western.

As the tour continued, John had a good look at the
Dean. Dean Littlegas was spoken of as one of the faculty's Young Turks, but he looked to John neither young
nor capable of toting a scimitar; he seemed gentle, he was
almost totally bald, and he wore odd-ball spectacles, with
metal-rimmed lenses which were rather small and perfectly circular, so that he seemed to be peering at the
world through a couple of stamp-collector's magnifying
glasses. The Dean was famous on the campus for having a
speech impediment—namely, whenever he opened his
mouth a little frog jumped out, in the form of a cliché. It
was well known that you could soften the bulletins of
adversity, when being harangued by Dr. Littlegas, by
playing a mental game known as Anticipating the Dean.

The Dean sat down, picked up and opened a manila
folder, and set off without clearing his throat.

—— Fist, I've been riffling through your folder. (I
should have known, John thought, that he would say
riffling.) You've been having something of a slump,
haven't you? Cutting classes right and left? I'm going to
suggest a remedy to you: Why don't you take a year off—
think things through?

John was just reflecting that, sleepy or not, this was
the one idea he would never have anticipated, when the
Dean went on:

—— You're a little bit taken aback to hear me throw
that one at you? I have to tell you, Fist, dropping out isn't
regarded as a heinous crime around here any more. We
actively solicit it. (I'm drowsy, I must be more alert, John

thought: heinous crime, actively solicit—inevitable.) Of the million two hundred thousand young people who entered colleges in this country last year, fifty-five per cent are destined to drop—

John quickly thought: —— By the wayside.

—— by the wayside. So we make the best of a bad job and encourage dropping out. Whenever I run across a chap whose motivation is—

—— At a low ebb.

—— at a low ebb, I don't hesitate to recommend a little time to—

—— Recharge the batteries.

—— recharge the batteries. Here at Sheldon, we have the expectation, with each class, of losing—

—— Something like.

—— something in the order of . . .

John, out loud: —— Damn!

—— twenty-five per cent. What was that you said, Fist?

—— Nothing, sir. I just hate the idea of leaving.

—— You do and you don't. Unconsciously you have been trying to flunk out in recent weeks. Look here! You got a D from Sylvian Orreman. That's well-nigh impossible—but it's still not a failing mark. Stopping classes dead is easy to do, and many try it. Actually flunking out is hard work, Fist, you have to dig in and—

—— Apply yourself.

—— apply yourself. The male adolescent often needs a—

—— Moratorium.

—— moratorium. Down through (Too easy, John thought) history, various cultures have provided various devices for young men to reshuffle and organize their powers. The monastery. Rabelais was a monk for a while.

So was Erasmus. The vows of youth don't have to be eternal. The Laboratory. The doctorate. Think of young Darwin sailing the seas on *The Beagle*. Young people grow—

———— In spurts.

———— in waves, and you have to ride the waves.

John, to himself this time: ———— Double damn.

Now John realized, through the mist of his lethargy, that in the very act of playing a game he had become boiling mad. How dared this oaf suggest that he do just what he was thinking of doing?

What made it infuriating was that the oaf had power. John hated bossism, and this guy, pretending to be a healer, was pure boss. He saw how Dean Littlegas sucked the life out of students, his own inner vitality deriving from the sense of power he got from manipulating young human beings. Baker, grow fat upon the kneading of thy dough! John saw the humble-seeming Dean as an undercover positivist, secretly an Ayn Rand type, a Me-Firster, believing in the survival, not necessarily of the fittest and certainly not of the best, but of the shrewdest and best-situated. He hid his self-serving autocracy in these thickets of clichés, and in his little bursts of solicitude. His dictatorship was capricious and irresponsible: throw this student out, pardon this one, advise this one to take a year off—all the while banking on the resilience of youth to compensate for errors in his judgment, lapses that might prove to have been almost criminal. His guideline was what would work, his test was getting away with it. A person was not supposed to live, he was supposed to function.

———— There's so much careerism around these days (Dr. Littlegas was saying), so much pressure to count credits, so much competition getting into post-graduate schools, so great a need to play it safe (John decided with some regret that he was too furious, and at the same time, oddly, too sleepy, to go on with the game of Anticipation), that what happens? It gets to be fun to run away. Students can only relax when they're in flight. Sports cars. Or, if it's inappropriateness one wants, a bum's life. Anything that gives a feeling that one is off the assembly line, free to wander, to choose. Free to kill time instead of making the best use of it. I suppose that's what this latest caper of yours was about.

John yawned—an involuntary tactical error. He had a strange feeling that Breed had put the yawn in his mouth.

—— I mean (a look of surprise and annoyance on the face of Dr. Littlegas) landing yourself in the clink. You'll forgive us for considering that slightly out of bounds. I'm willing to write it off, this once, Fist, to pursuit of a negative identity fragment. That's why I'm suggesting some time off—time for you to find at least a tentative ego identity that makes sense for you. Something balancing out the dynamic polarities: stay or go, compete or pitch in, conform or rebel, short trim or Beatle bangs. (John realized he was missing some big chances.) A matter of tuning up your strings. Leaving this way can require courage, but——

John, ever more furious, felt his eyelids drooping. To keep himself awake he yawned again—this time a delicious engagement of muscles all the way down to his breastbone.

That was it. Dean Littlegas looked (as he himself might have said) about to go up in smoke. He stood up and bit off a command:

—— Think it over, Fist, when you next find yourself fully awake.

21

Dear Fam:

For once I am trying to be dead level with you, so please don't just skip through this letter. I AM SINCERE. Believe me.

Now. Hang on to your back teeth for a minute. Please be patient and read to the end. I'm thinking of leaving Sheldon. I haven't looked far enough ahead yet to have decided whether I'll come back after a year or two off, one thing at a time. Look, the point is I've felt as if a steamroller was just one grunt behind me ever since kindergarten: Make Sheldon. Get into Sheldon. So I got in. But now that I'm here I find that's not the end of the pavement by any means. (There are a thousand ideas I'd like to be getting down, mixed up in this, I'm only really scratching the surface.) I have to go on to more of

151

this incredible grind. I was thinking a bit about maybe eventually working for a paper or a magazine —until the other day I heard that at Contact, *as you know one of the real great ones to work for, they'll accept you for office boy or mailroom with a B.A., but if you have any idea of being an editor or a writer, you have to have at the very least an M.A. Balls to that.*

And yet that's not the most important part of it. I just feel as if I don't have it. I can't complain about Sheldon—quite the opposite. This is a terrific place, and the trouble is that I'm not worthy of it—not putting one tenth into the place that it deserves.

I don't know, I have a feeling of being hung up as your son. I can't express this too well, but I guess I'll never shake the feeling that I got in here on a legacy, and on top of that I feel as if I'm not on my own, because after all you foot the bills. I can't even have a Coke without thinking it's your dime.

You know something? I've never experienced poverty. Not that we're all that rich—but I mean true poverty. I envy poor people right to the marrow of my bones. And I'll tell you something crazier than that. I've never had a war—the way you did, Pop. I envy people who know what a war was like. Leaving Sheldon can at least take a little courage, and maybe that's part of it.

By the way, Father dear, everyone around here says your war, or its aftermath anyway, disproved once and for all that there was anything sacred about going through Sheldon in four years. They all say that the ones who came back after being away did better than anybody, including themselves before.

I've sort of stopped going to classes. I don't know exactly why. I didn't mind them so much. I thought old Orreman was first-rate, and there's a guy named Gutwillig who apart from being a kind of a pincher where young girls are concerned has a mind like a Ferrari engine, and it's a pleasure to hear it purr along. I don't know, I can't exactly say I wasn't interested. It just seems too far to walk to class a lot of the time.

I feel as if I want to get outside myself. I'm sick of me. I'm really up to the teeth with being a member of the brightest college generation ever to enter Sheldon, when I feel so stupid, so sleepy, so much of the time. You don't think I believe in anything whatsoever, but I think (God, I really am trying to be Straight With You) I think I do. Not in a cause. In fact, what I believe in is a cause inside out, in a way. I can't dedicate my life to capitalism or liberalism or socialism or communism or conservatism or quietism or positivism or any other ism: I think it's too late for politics in those old-fashioned senses. It seems insane to me to fight a war in Vietnam to Stop Communism. That isn't what it's about, anyway. I buy Edmund Wilson's sea-slug theory—that nations are primitive cannibalistic organisms that have only one basic drive: eat each other up. The same is basically true of human individuals—only they literally can't stomach each other. Oh God, what am I trying to say? I guess I'm trying to say that I disagree very fundamentally with you about what our lives should be about on this earth. It's too dangerous to go on in the old way. But—my final honesty with you for today—I'm not clear about the new way. I want some time to look for it, to look around, and be, and think.

There, I have come clean—in a most inarticulate and inadequate way. But we've had such a hard time talking lately that I thought it might be better to try to write it down. Sorry it's so abrupt. I mean it, though.

Love (mean that too)
John

22

Two days after mailing the letter John got a telegram:
CALL HOME TONIGHT LOVE MOTHER AND FATHER.

Out of self-respect John waited overnight and the next evening called from the glass booth at the corner of Planique and Ash from which he had first phoned Margaret. He reversed the charges; it was their money anyway.

His mother's voice: —— Yes?

This salutation had always been a source of annoyance to John. Why couldn't she say hello like anyone else?

John: —— Hi. It's me.

Mother: —— Hold on a minute.

Some greeting to long-lost son! John felt like kicking himself for having been so open in his letter. Long pause. Then click.

Father: —— O.K. I'm on. Hello, John-boy.

Mother: —— We all want to be in on this. Your father's on the extension in the kitchen. (Powerful self-control reverberating in her voice, making it sound like the other end of a bad connection.)

Malcolm Fist on that wall-fixture extension beside the clipboard for grocery lists. John was on the edge of saying the woman's place is in the—

Mother, the connection becoming all too good: —— How could you do this to us? After all we've tried to do for you all these years?

Father: —— Now, Mom. We agreed—

Mother: —— Stop censoring me with my own son! I think I'm entitled to an answer. All those years of planning and . . . and . . . (unspoken word: scrimping) when the whole point in life was Sheldon College for . . . for the male child who had the I.Q. to do it.

Father: —— Look, Rowena, let me talk to him for a minute.

Mother: —— Oh, sure, you talk. You're the one who talked nothing but Sheldon Sheldon Sheldon for twenty years.

John: —— Why don't I call back tomorrow night at the same time?

Father: —— Son, have you discussed this with anyone? Have you talked to the Dean?

John, feeling himself tighten up: —— I have.

Mother: —— How will you ever get a decent job? Who would hire somebody who started out by . . . (unspoken word vivid in the pause: quitting)—

Father: —— What did the Dean say?

John: —— He said, Blessings on thee, barefoot boy.

Mother: —— I should think this would be the one time in your life when you could be serious.

John: —— No, Mom, the one time has already been. When I wrote that letter the other day.

John had an uneasy feeling, however, that his mother was calming down, gathering her forces. She had let out the bottled-up hysteria of two days, and now she was going to zero in. Then John had a moment of absolute clarity, and of awful prevision: his father would go to pieces in a minute, and then it would be his own turn after that.

But now his father said quite coolly: —— Can you tell us what's really eating you—what's really behind this?

John, very careful: —— It's like I said in the letter. I can't see that the feasts of learning they spread out around here have any connection with the real world. Every once in a while a course will dance right up to the edge of an issue that's really relevant, and then foof, it dodges, just runs out on us.

Mother: —— Then you mean (ooh, the easy tone of that voice now) that you're disappointed in your father's alma mater?

John: —— No, not really. I think it's my fault really. In spite of what I just said, Sheldon is too good for me. I think if I were a bit older, let's say more experienced, maybe I could live up to the place.

Father: —— Isn't it a matter of trying to decide who you are? (And yes, John thought he could detect an incipient tremor in his father's voice underlying the palship, the understanding.) Isn't it a mild case of identity diffusion?

John: —— Oh for God's sake, Pop, not that. You're

making like a Dean. Dean Littlegas filled me full of that Erik Erikson crap.

Father: —— I didn't see a war, John. I never got near the war. The closest I got was Pearl Harbor—big air-conditioned office, rum swizzles at the Halekulani, you could hear the starch crackle when you put on the white uniforms. Why didn't you ever *ask* me about the war?

John: —— I guess because I wanted to spare your delicate feelings.

Father (one long groan of a sentence): —— What did we do that was wrong?

Mother: —— Son, we talked to Dr. Stempleman yesterday. . . .

The headshrinker with a pretty good housewife trade on the "edge" of Worcester. John's flash reaction to the name was to think of the day he'd gone to see Dr. Barnes, the Sheldon Health Department psychiatrist, after he'd had a bout of nerves midway through freshman year. What stood out in John's memory from a great deal else that may have made sense was the doc's saying: —— When you're forty, you may have a certain ruddiness the day after intercourse. John remembered wondering what professor's wife the doctor was banging, to make him say such a kookie thing as that. Anyway, the doc had given him some phenobarb, and life had turned out to be fine.

John: —— What was that, Mom?

Mother: —— He said, why don't you take a weekend and come up and talk things out?

Suddenly John, realizing that his turn had come, was gripped by fear.

John: —— I can't, I have to stay here.

Mother: —— What do you mean, son? In one sentence you talk about dropping out, and in the next—

John: —— I'm in trouble. I made a deal . . .

Mother (solid response to a shout for help): —— Tell me what this is about.

John: —— There's a guy named Breed. . . .

Father (completely out of hand; going off like a fire-cracker): —— Is he a homo?

John: —— Oh God, no. It's nothing like that. He's . . . he's trying to . . . to close in on me.

Mother: —— Is it blackmail? What's this about? You'll have to—

But John hung up the phone.

23

WHEN Breed finally turned up at John's room, a couple of nights later, very late, so late that Flack was already an inert heap on his bed across from John's desk, John felt no fear, but only relief, curiosity, and a mild excitement like that of sitting in a theater as the lights go down.

Breed pulled Flack's desk chair over near John's and they talked in murmurs so as not to waken the horrible roommate.

Breed: —— Long time no see. How's it going?

John: —— What do you mean *it*? Not a bloody particle of *it* has happened. In fact, everything is so nothing that I've told David Littlegas, Esquire, that I'm going to split. Leave him, this—and you. You and your crappy piece of paper, among other things.

—— Have you told your parents?

—— Yes.

—— Roof fall in?

—— Three guesses.

—— But that wasn't a breakthrough?

—— Oh God no, it was just frustrating like every-thing else. Brother, your big deal—you really cut me a slice of salami.

—— You've had it?

—— I've had the whole bargain. To the uttermost teeth.

—— Great. I knew it, but I'm glad to hear you speak with conviction for once. Now listen carefully to me, John Fist. (Suddenly, for the first time in weeks, John became aware of the short-circuit smell, and his heart began to jump.) Our twenty-six weeks are almost up. I've pur-posely let you flounder all this time so you'd be thor-oughly ripe. Ripe and ready. Up to now you haven't had the breakthroughs you wanted or done my organization any good, either. Now I'm going to take you in hand, and you're really going to fly.

Breed made a kind of hissing sound, and in the dim glow of John's little desk lamp John saw that Breed's jaws were set and his lips drawn back in what might have been a smile but might also have been a grimace of effort, or pain, or distaste.

—— Fly?

—— I'm going to take you on a trip through experi-ence.

—— How does that work?

—— You've been letting life happen to you. I'm going to make you become what you do.

Breed paused, evidently to let John think about that.

John: —— Breakthroughs?

—— You bet.

—— And—

—— And *our* work. I'll say!

Ozone, ozone! Once again John felt himself being caught up in a huge vague field of force in which something had gone unutterably haywire. But this time he felt joyful, and he let himself sink into the odor, the disorder, and the sense of power, and he said:

—— At last.

Breed, now rather businesslike: —— The reason you've felt frustrated is that you've wanted the impossible without knowing how to attain it: not all or nothing, but all *and* nothing at the same time. You wanted to be an absolute anonymity but also wanted to be treated as Somebody Special. Minor disagreements meant nothing to you, but at the same time you felt free to construe the very ones that meant least to you as outright treason; especially where your ma was concerned. You shrugged off doubts but thought of the very ones that were most shruggable as portents of the Apocalypse. You wanted to live by both existentialism and idealism at the same time. You wanted to be *alive*, to assert your right to a living life; but you wanted quiescence, too, the right to resign, pull out—not be. We'll find a meeting ground for all these incongruities in the next few days and nights.

—— How? What do you mean?

—— First of all, we're going to have to reorient you in time. You've been trying to live entirely in the present, because you felt the past was irrelevant and the future would be too bad to think about. Now we're going to sharpen up the present, really shoot the moon in the present tense, but it's going to be as fierce as it is partly because the meaning of the past will be all scrambled up in it, and the possibilities for the future, too.

—— All right, but how?

—— I'm going to give you powers you've never imagined. At times you'll be—*possessed.*

John was interested, observing himself, that he still
felt no fear. He was overcome by a lethargy of a sort that
was new to him—willingness.

Breed went on: —— What have you wanted most of
all? What if not those very things that have seemed most
unattainable? Forbidden fruit. Whenever you've spoken
of wanting "experiences," what you've really wanted has
been to go way out, hasn't it?—right out to the most
dizzying edges. I'm going to help you to do that. You'll
experience new and different things, all right—to the
bloody hilt. Then we'll see if you think of my contract as
a cheat. . . .

Breed's hushed promises made John want to shout
hosannahs and hurrahs. He felt that his chest would burst
with delight, impatience.

Flack stirred and groaned, as if John actually had let
out an unearthly yip.

Breed, after a pause to let Flack go under again:
—— You've put yourself really at my mercy, you know,
John, because you've rejected a whole set of rules for life
without finding anything to take their place. We'll go
look for a new set. O.K.?

—— When do we start?

—— I don't guarantee that we'll find a new set.

—— When?

—— Tomorrow night. Midnight.

BOOK THREE

BOOK THREE

24

A CLOUD blew across the half moon; it was as if the houses set back from the street were all at once covered with fur. The pair walked at an unhurried pace on soft soles. Breed had specified sneakers, and John felt his springy tennis shoes communicating a lithe rubberiness all up through his musculature, so that his heels, the balls of his feet, his calves, his thighs, his hams, and even his waist and arms were all smoothly engaged in his silent, fluent movement along a side street of Sheldon town.

John looked up at a street lamp, a glowing ridged glass globe at the undercurve of which a cemetery of moths made a dark circle, repeated large on the pavement below. A telephone pole stood close by in the thrown light, with splinter-fringed holes rammed into its creosote-soaked pine by the climbing irons of linemen; Breed had said that there would be an ascent tonight, and he had brought nylon rope and a steel grapnel. He wore the coil of rope looped on one shoulder, like an aide's aiguillette —a set of those loops of braided colored cord that John had once heard a Marine call chicken guts. John carried the cold hook.

The light of the lamps picked out a street sign at the top of a silvery-painted pipe post: ASH STREET.

John knew that Ash Street led down to Cruel Creek. Gutwillig had suggested once, back in the fall term, that his lecturees go take a look at the Cruel Creek area, and John, then obedient, had obeyed. Pincher Gutwillig had called it Sheldon Township's upstairs ghetto, worth glomming. The focal point was Dortman Street, a narrow, curving gorge of wooden frame buildings of four and five stories which at ground level housed dingy artisan shops —shoe repair, furniture mending, watch repair, tailoring —and small specialized stores where fish, candy, pizzas, fruit and vegetables, delicatessen, cheap dry goods, liquor, and household items were sold; the owners of these establishments, sons and grandsons of immigrant Italians, Poles, and European Jews, also owned the rickety stacks of wooden rooms upstairs and rented them out, now, exclusively to Negroes. This, as Pincher G. had pointed out, set the pattern of friction in Sheldon. Each building was known as a tenement block—the Pozzi block, the Goldman block, the Kowalski block, the Carraggiolo block, and so on. The side of the street on the outer rim of the curve backed hard against Cruel Creek, which was called that because of the way it had boiled up after the autumn torrents brought inland by a century's worth of hurricanes. After its last uprising, which had threatened the underpinnings of several tenement blocks, the Army Engineers had come in and lined its banks with big cracked rocks, so now it was a glorified ditch.

The two men were silent as they walked down Ash Street. John asked no questions. The moon was out again, and in the milky light John saw a queer house with a round tower at one corner, and he was aware of a sudden evocation of Grampa Newson; windowseats, a moldy smell, wicker furniture, tennis rackets with broken strings —a strong whiff of a secure, complacent past time.

A cat, silent too, scurried across the street ahead.

They walked four blocks and then were at the dead end of Dortman. Here, upstairs, were a few lights and muffled sounds: laughter, the cavernous thumping of TV voices. Breed crossed to the far sidewalk and turned left. About a hundred paces along, the pair came to an alley-way cutting in to the right between two tenement blocks, and Breed swung into it; John followed. The darkness in the alley seemed thick and chilly, and entering it was almost like going into water. Underfoot: loose rubble, wads of paper, tin cans. John put out a hand and touched a wall—damp, clammy.

They came out into a dirty, narrow yard, where the moonlight seemed dry and dazzling. At the far end stood a shoulder-high wooden fence. At some distance beyond, over the fence, loomed the cold rectangles of factory backs.

Breed leaped, pulled, got a knee up on the fence top, and wriggled over, and John did the same, parking the grapnel on the crest of the fence while he went over, then retrieving it.

They were just above the man-made bank of Cruel Creek. Breed started off to the right, along behind the tenement blocks. At first they walked in dead weeds along the edge of the stone facing of the Creek, but soon

the buildings and the fence crowded tighter and tighter
against the embankment, and the pair had to move down
and along the steeply slanting split-rock bank. There was
a vile smell here, of sewage in the Creek and rotting filth
dumped on the slope. The footing was hazardous—sharp-
edged stones the size of anvils, crumpled trash, slimy
heaps of God knew what.

Looking up, John saw the curious backs of the
houses. Every one had a series of sagging, rickety wooden
balconies, one to each floor, fenced with thin-spindled
balustrades and roofed at the very top. The balconies did
not connect from house to house, and in fact were at
varying levels and were walled from each other. Across at
the other side of the Creek was a series of factories and
warehouses, huge, ponderous, rectilinear, their half-lit
brick-and-concrete solidity properous-looking compared
with the crazed wooden tenements. Between, at the foot
of the vee of the embankments, the moon sparkled on the
face of the Creek, its water shallow now, rippling around
old smooth-shouldered rocks; the moon-fire on the water
almost made one forget its stinking burden of ordure.

Breed stooped. He put a hand on John's arm, and
with his other hand he pointed upward. He inclined his
head close to John's and said very softly:

—— Carraggiolo block. Top floor. They're very poor.
You go up. I'll wait here.

Even here in the open air, dominating the stench of
the Creek and the garbage, there came into John's nostrils
the smell he associated with Breed, with challenge, with
calculation far swifter than thought, the odor of modern
times gone awry. John's heart had begun to race. Somehow he knew what he was going to do, and he began to
rock with laughter which he realized might quickly get
out of hand; but Breed gripped his arm hard and said:

—— Shhh. Don't be an idiot. You'd better get going.

Breed thrust the coil of rope into one of John's hands and then said:

—— Wait a second.

He reached in a trouser pocket and came out with a little cylinder, which he gave to John, a flashlight, John realized, the size of a fountain pen. He pocketed it.

John scaled the fence and dropped into an enclosure which was like a miniature junkyard. There was a dim light on the ground floor; perhaps someone was in the store, perhaps a light was left burning as a precaution. John tried to advance as quietly as a rat across heaps of broken and rusted and decomposing items that once must have been cherished by people upstairs, but soon he stepped on an old half-buried and half-corroded coffeepot or cooking boiler, which collapsed under his weight with a loud cranky noise. At once John heard the sound of a screen door slamming high on one of the balconies. He crouched, head down, in order not to throw a man's shadow, and froze. A long silence. He stood up and in four quick bounds was under the edge of the balconies.

The building had five stories, and John saw why Breed had brought the rope and iron: Whereas the up-stairs balconies were supported by posts which stood at the very rims of the porches, and so could be climbed from one level to another, the lowest balcony was held up by metal stanchions set a couple of feet back from the edge; skinning up one of them would only bring a climber up against an overhanging soffit.

There seemed to be a trapdoor leading up to the first balcony, but it apparently could not be reached or opened from below—was probably there so a fire-escape ladder could be let down from above.

John tied one end of the rope to the ring of the four-pronged hook. For a few minutes he looked for a pole, something with which to raise the grapnel and avoid the noise of throwing it even a short distance, but he could find nothing. He took aim for a spot alongside one of the balcony posts and heaved the iron. It went too high and looped over the wooden railing with a terrible clatter.

John ducked out of the moonlight under the balcony. He listened with alert ears. He heard Fats Waller somewhere singing "Your Feet's Too Big." A catbird—could it be, late in March? Or was it Breed encoding laughter from beyond the fence?

Very slowly John took up on the nylon line, until it grew taut, and moving out again he gradually put more and more weight on the rope. Would the railing up there hold? The hook seemed to be engaged right next to the pillar, but everything here looked so sagging, so dry-rotted and discouraged.

But now he hung safely from the rope off the ground, and he went up quickly hand over hand. He felt a great lightness, a wild exuberance; he wanted to make a crazy answering catbird call, but he kept silent.

He got one hand up on the lip of the flooring of the balcony above, and then, letting go of the rope, the other hand, and he chinned himself over the edge to take a look; suddenly Fats Waller was giving his piano a much louder walk—a light from the window. Someone was in these rooms.

Letting himself down at arm's length, John handed himself along to the near end of the balcony, where, once up, he would be in shadow. He reached up to the rail, which creaked—he paused—and then he pulled himself upward, got a knee on the edge, and soon was standing on the balcony against the end wall.

John undid the hook from the line, set the iron gently

down, and wrapped the rope again and again around his waist until he could tie the ends; he had decided he would need the rope.

Then, seeing a wooden fire-escape ladder lowered from the next balcony, he thought: —— This is going to be too easy.

It turned out not. John ran on tiptoe across the squeaking porch and swiftly went up the ladder, getting a sidelong glimpse in a window of a Negro boy of about fifteen on his spine in an easy chair, stockinged heels outstretched on linoleum, reading under an upright lamp with thread fringe on its shade. The music was loud beside the boy: no one in there would hear anything. But when he reached the next balcony, where the windows were dark, John saw that there was no ladder farther up.

Exulting in the strength and lack of fear of an energumen, John climbed a balcony post and hauled himself up to the fourth-floor porch.

Here in a room lighted by a bare bulb that hung down from the ceiling on a twisted wire, John saw an old Negro man, with a hat on, frying something over an electric ring; blue smoke was rising from the frying pan, and the man was bouncing a fork by its tines on the edge of the table that held the hot plate.

John's elation was almost unbearable. He wanted to watch the man eat in the middle of the night, he salivated just speculating about the smell of the smoke—but he tore himself from the window, grasped a post, swung outward, and began to shinny up to the last balcony.

Halfway up John abruptly felt abandoned, drained. Without warning, all the strange infused strength of the last few minutes had left him. Bitterly exhausted, all at once, from the climbing he had already done, he clutched the pillar with his arms and legs, just to hold on, just to keep from peeling off and falling. His upper arms began to cramp. He closed his eyes, giddy at the thought of how high he was. He felt such sharp pains in his hands and arms that for a few moments he was beside himself, not himself at all; his attention was so clamped to his agony that he seemed to slide outside his student self, to escape from all his boredom, his frustration, his anger, his bewilderment, so that in his most piercing discomfort he felt a never-before-experienced peace. Sweet, excruciating corporal penance! John was fascinated, even though in an extremity of danger, by the intensity of his feelings in all directions. If he survived, would he look back on this crisis, he wondered, as a breakthrough? Was a breakthrough only something to be felt in retrospect?

But then an out-of-season catbird sang down by the Creek, and all that inner turbulence, that pain, fear, and triumphant calm, floated away, and the strength was suddenly there again, and he climbed easily onto the topmost level.

Fresh from that appalling (yet thrilling) loss of his abnormal strength and regaining of it, John now felt like a panther, graceful, silent, and threatening. He swung a leg over the final railing and moved into the balcony's cave of moon-shadow. At once, glancing at a window, he saw that although the room on the balcony side was dark, there were lights beyond; lines of light ran around an inner door that was not shut tight. Someone was at home and awake.

John unwound the rope from his waist and coiled it and laid it quietly on the porch floor.

He tried the door that came out to the balcony; it was locked.

Over the windows were screens, evidently left on the

year round. John chose the window closest to the more shadowed end of the porch. With the briefest peep of the pen-sized flashlight he saw that the flange of the window lock was not engaged with its partner. He removed his belt, and using the tongue of the buckle he began to break the fly-screen wires along the frame. Breaking and entering: he savored the phrase. He had to work slowly; even these rusty wires made a twanging sound as they gave way.

At last he was able to turn up enough of a flap of wire to admit his body. The window had to be raised with great patience and care; once it gave out a shocking stuttery bumping sound.

John slid into the room.

At once he could hear voices in the next room. Treble and bass. Several. His scalp and buttocks crawled with his excitement.

He could see by reflected moonlight that he was in a bedroom. An iron bedstead. Bureau. Mirror. Pictures. A treadle sewing machine.

A round of laughter from the next room—rather sedate. John was helplessly drawn to the door where the lines of lights showed. He stood close against it, listening.

He distinguished, in time, five or six voices. That one man's voice! Hadn't he heard it somewhere before? A woman spoke, a fluty tone. Then the man again. Phrases: it was serious talk. He heard a woman speak of the President, accent on the last syllable, putting teeth in the high office. Then the man, talking about Title Two of some bill. . . .

Holy smoke! The voice belonged to Dom Faglio.

John dropped to one knee and looked through the keyhole, intensely listening as he peeked. Since the door was not shut tight, the hole was not aimed squarely across

the way, and John saw a bit of one side of a corridorlike
space and most of a keyhole-shaped segment of a sitting
room. Exactly framed in the bright space was a light-
brown woman of about thirty, facing John, in a rocker.
Her dress was brown, darker than her skin, of some sort
of rough twill, grease-spotted and painfully shabby. John
sensed that these were her rooms. Her hair had been
ironed, but not lately; it daggered off to the rear. Her face
was a heavy-lined lithograph on which the cutting acid
must have been self-pity. She dropped her eyes as Faglio
spoke; John felt that dignity was struggling against an
adverse judgment of some kind. Then she spoke: spoke of
the Movement. Listening and seeing the lips, John understood that this was some group laying plans for a response in Sheldon Township to the implementation of
some aspect of the anti-poverty program, if and when.
Dom Faglio spoke the phrase Indigenous People rever-
ently, so it sounded unconsciously condescending. The
woman nodded, as if to say, yes yes yes it's all so familiar.

As he watched and listened John felt swelling within
him again, to an almost unbearable pitch, those feelings
he had had clutching the porch post, going in all directions. He fought an impulse to throw his head back and
laugh; yet he was aware of the danger he was in; yet at
the same time he had a desire, so intense as to make his
hot eyes smart with a need for tears which would never
come, never, a desire that things could be more nearly
right with the world—or even just with this woman who
had such cruel frown marks between her eyebrows. He
was going to steal her blind. He wanted the terrible
dragon he saw in the pools of her eyes to be lanced, or be
eased. But he was going to strip her of everything that
mattered to her. His heart hammered at his neck. There

174

could be nothing more vile than what he was going to do. She crossed her legs; the skirt caught, and the line going up her thighs was long. Rape? A silk stocking around a light-brown neck? A match to this tinderbox? No! His burglary would be far more despicable. How could he keep from roaring with laughter? He actually put a hand to his throat to keep the shattering ebullience down.

Was that a catbird's meow? John jumped to his panther feet and went to work.

On the bedside table was an ancient radio; the pen-flashlight, winking a moment, lit up the jigsaw-carved. fretwork of its speaker. John unplugged the set, took it to the window, placed it out on the balcony.

He leaped to the sewing machine, worked the drive belt off the big wheel below by the treadle, undid the wing nuts under the fabric table, and lifted off the machine, which smelled strongly of 3-in-1 Oil. He put it outside.

Then he stole many smaller things. He stripped the pillowcase from the single pillow on the bed and began to drop objects into it. A picture from the bureau top (blinked at by the flashlight) of a dark-faced boy in a white sailor suit, aged about twelve. From within the top drawer, a cloisonné box of brooches and pins. A dish of pennies. A bottle of pills. He had a sense, rummaging in high spirits, not only of the most careful frugality here but also of a burning pride. In the underwear drawer, from which he drew out only the false-satiny things at one side, there were sachets of herbs; he took them. Hidden under some clothing he found a packet of letters tied with grocer's string; he took them. Behind a hanging cloth in the corner which served for a closet, he found, among many stale-smelling rags, one presentable dress;

he stuffed it in the pillowcase. On a glass shelf over a washbasin: a diaphragm and a tube of jelly; a jar of hair goo; an electric hot comb.

Heavy steps in the corridor, coming toward the bedroom!

John pranced behind the curtain, and his fear and exuberance were tremendous. He heard a door open, heard urination, heard a toilet flushed. The steps went back.

John slipped out and, using the flashlight, began to inspect the baseboards and the linoleum-covered floor. Under the bed, lifting an edge of the linoleum where crease marks showed it had often been lifted, he found what he was looking for: a short length of loose floorboard. He pried one end up, removed it, reached down. A soft bag. He opened its throat and felt the touch of a slim roll of bills, and coins. A blip of the flashlight: an insurance premium; burial-society papers; a Social Security card. He put all these things in the pillowcase.

He slid out the window, tied the rope through the wheel of the sewing machine, stood up, and with the flashlight signaled downward the Morse code letter B: dash dot dot dot. He wanted to guffaw at the realization that he had learned the Morse code as a Boy Scout, and he thought: God, I should have told Mona I only missed Eagle by three merit badges.

Again: dash dot dot dot.

A catbird sang in the junkyard below. John began to let the rope down.

25

BREED's hand hovered over the coffee table, and at the exact center of the surface his thumb and forefinger parted. A capsule dropped onto the waxed wood.

Breed: —— All of Paradise, in such a tiny compass.

John: —— I'll bet. And Styx and Tartarus and Erebus, too. Right? And Acheron and the Lake of the Dead. Right?

—— Lysergic acid diethylamide. One hundred micrograms, or one ten-thousandth of a gram, fleshed out with plain sugar. When you take an aspirin, you take five grams. This little baby, in other words, has one fifty-thousandth as much dose as an aspirin tablet has. But in experience—infinity. The closest equivalent to infinity in sheer living. Take it, friend. Want some water for a chaser?

—— Wait a minute. I want to know more about what to expect.

—— Experiences, old John. The onset will come from fifteen minutes to an hour after ingestion. The experiences will reach a plateau—and what a lofty one, what a Xanadu!—after about an hour and a half. They'll start to recede after four hours and be altogether finished in six to twelve hours. That's it.

—— You say experiences . . .

—— Ah, John, they're for you to make and have. I can't describe what's in you to create.

John looked at the big, square, white-faced electric clock on the desk, its long second hand sweeping around and around like an inexorable wiper of existence. How fast it went! Seventeen minutes past eleven in the morning. If what Breed said was true, it would be all over before midnight; part of one day to live through infinity. A wave of bitter curiosity, then one of extreme excitement, washed over John.

—— O.K. I'm game. Yes. I'd like some water to wash it down.

Those steel ball bearings behind Breed's wire-rimmed glasses seemed actually, for a briefest instant, to grow so brightly hot as to give off smoke—or at least to be capable of giving off smoke—but then Chum's head was turned away as he rose to go to the bathroom for water. He seemed to trail eddies of hypnotic influence after him. John was used to those importunate looks now, and did not feel, as once he might have felt, that he should be taking warning.

Breed offered him a dirty toothbrush glass half filled with water. John picked up the little capsule, examined it, popped it in his mouth, and took two swallows of water. He laughed. It was as easy as that to commit himself to an infinity of experiences.

Breed: —— There! Lucky fellow. . . . Now listen. Whatever happens, don't be afraid. I'm going to be right here with you.

—— Couldn't you have brought up the being afraid part before I took the stuff?

—— An oversight. *Mea culpa.*

—— Brother.

But John could not dwell on worries; he was euphoric. They were in Breed's cheerful room. Brilliant sunlight poured in the diamond-paned windows. Overhead, outside those windows, was an inverted glazed blue casserole of a sky that seemed to have been scrubbed just for this occasion with Old Dutch Cleanser. Breed had fixed up his single room with a few touches that made it glow on a day like this: curtains of a red worthy of a vest, two black armchairs with cushions of the same red, the coffee table with bright ash trays, and, near the center, near where the capsule had rested, a little metaphor of a crowded world: three small glass pigs sealed one within another. On the walls were prints of op art—a thing, by someone you never heard of, of multicolored candy canes that began, if you let your eyes go, to revolve like a score of barber poles, and a festoon of Möbius bands, and a beautiful, serene Albers, pale, harmonious squares within squares that seemed to ease one's mind about the pig metaphor.

The clock hands wiped along. Breed and John chatted. Suddenly the Munson Memorial Carillon in the tower of the Forrestal Complex (glass bells recorded on tape, dropped three octaves and amplified by a factor of seventy) played, according to the unbreakable terms of

the Munson bequest, the theme of *"Parigi, o cara,"* from
La Traviata. Noon.

—— You bastard (John said), you gave me a lousy
placebo. Nothing's happening.

—— Relax, friend.

And John did relax. He put one hand on each arm of
the black armchair, stretched out his legs, and laid his
head back against the curved headrest, and by a gradual
flow of warmth in his limbs he began to know that something was in truth ahold of him—something big, majestic,
full of the stirring promise of April. He saw the ceiling
bright with reflected sunlight and tinged palest pink by
the glow of the red curtains. As if great chords were
modulating in him, he felt slow progressions from a
pleasant looseness in all his muscles, to a dissolving of
tension, to a relaxation of his conscience, to a deep tran-
quillity, to, at last, an indescribable, time-stopping calm
at the very core of his being.

He sighed and said gratefully to Breed: —— It's
begun.

—— Isn't it wonderful?

John nodded, or thought he nodded, or thought he
would like to nod. Such a sweet lassitude had come over
him that he did not know whether there was any discern-
ible line between thought and action. To test this, he
thought he would raise his head from the backrest of the
chair, and now, slowly, slowly, his field of vision did indeed change: eventually he was looking out the window.

Then he was struck by what seemed to him the most
beautiful sight he had ever seen.

The line at the window's edge between the vest-red
of the curtain and the bowl-glaze-blue of the sky seemed
to soften, melt, blur, until what had been a razor's edge of
color change had become a glorious effulgence, a misty

radiance that compromised the two primaries in a glow of regal purple. John thought of the passage about St. Elmo's fire in *Moby Dick*. One could only think of this shimmering rod of light as a manifestation of glory. God must have looked like this in the burning bush.

But wait! It was getting better! It had begun to breathe with John's breathing: the extent of the glow was stable, but the pigments breathed. Slowly, rhythmically, the magical incandescence went from purple to magenta to lilac to lavender to mauve to plum to fuchsia to orchid. And still, to either side, solid blue and solid red.

John, focusing his attention on the remarkable fact that the breathing of the colors coincided with his own breathing, thought: —— I am the bush, and the divinity is in me.

He closed his eyes. The purple rod was still there. It began to move, to undulate, to break up. Now John saw patterns of his inner omnipotence. The colors moved, both in space and in tone. All were dominated by the warmth of the marriage of curtain and sky, manifested in all those diaphanous purples. Tropics, a Guatemala of the secret self. Purple fronds of coconut slowly waved under a purple sea. Fish with shot-silk tails swam among the highest branches. Fans of coral, boughs of frangipani. Sea anemone and land anemone. Golden sponge and passion flower.

Nothing could be like this. Breed—where was Breed?—Breed had talked for days of all the other ways; but nothing could be like this. Not the nepenthe that Helen dropped in Telemachus' cup, nor the Pythoness's draughts of the underground stream, nor the breathing of the yogas, nor the self-tortures of the Sioux hanging in the sun by torn muscles, nor Persians' dreaming on *soma;* not *les Paradis artificiels, opium et haschisch;* not Roman

aconite and belladonna in love potions; not the witches'
ointment; not the fly-agaric mushroom nibbled by
nomads in frozen Siberia; not coca from the Andes, thorn
apple, mandrake, henbanes; not the psilocybe, teona-
nacatl, God's flesh; not curare, peyote, morning-glory;
not big H nor booze nor marijuana nor model airplane
glue. Not anything at all could be like this. The colors!

This was not believing in God yet having God in
one's veins.

Unbearably beautiful sounds. Had Breed turned on
his record player?

Now was heard by Johaanan all maner of Instruments of Musick, as Organs, Clarigolds, Lutes, Viols,
Citerns, Waights, Hornepipes, Fluites, Anomes, Harpes,
and all maner of other Instruments the which so rauished
his minde, that hee thought hee had been in another
Worlde, forgat both body and soule, in so much that he
was minded never to change his opinion concerning all
that he had done on this Earth. Come with me, come
with Johaanan Fistus, come and we will runne through
wals, doores, and gates of stone and yron, and we will
creep into the earth like wormes, we will swimme in the
water like fish, we will flie in the ayre like birds, and we
will live and nourish our selfes in the fire like Salaman-
ders; come, we will learne to go inuisible, we will finde
out the mines of golde and silver, the fodines of precious
stones, as the Carbuncle, the Diamond, Saphir, Emerald,
Rubie, Topas, Iacinct, Granat, Iaspis, Amathist, come, we
will use all these at our pleasure, we will take our hearts'
desire.

Each jewel could be seen in response to a musical
note, a drop of liquid music—all glow, all sparkle, white,
blue, green, red, yellow, showing stars, facets, glints. Still,
like a plasm of life, the warm and happy purples kept

coming back, taking over. Now not John's breathing but the music he heard set the rhythm of the shifts in color. A dancing kaleidoscope of *Eine Kleine Nachtmusik*. The silvery-gold-white-yellow dripping of harps and celesta with the presentation of the silver rose in *Der Rosenkavalier*.

But then: What had been that *we*? *We* will run through walls, take *our* hearts' desire.

Margaret. John and Margaret as the only we. Now John was aware of the presence with him of Margaret. She filled the room with her fragrance, her naïveté, her lying on her side on the motel bed with both hands flat under her cheek. She stood somewhere and held up her hands, offering something. She could not be seen or heard —the musicolors flew across John's eardrum-eyelids—but her being there was sure, solid, was almost but not quite touchable. John's delight was beyond bounds he had ever conceived possible.

Now there poured into him, as if one so full could be at the same time utterly empty, the most powerful feeling of aspiration—and with it came colored, chord-banging fireworks, brilliant against heavens that were not night-black but were on that glowing edge between curtain and sky. He thought: I want to be useful—and simultaneously this thought became visible: pinwheels! rockets! flashes of cherry bombs! colored sprays in the sky! And audible: Stravinsky! Still deeply aware of the innocence of Margaret all around him, John went through a kind of delirium of idealism.

Now this optimism, this yearning, so central to John's sense of youthfulness and of bursting health, began to grow branches. Both the thought and its visualization became complex, with cognates, qualifications, analogies, consequences, doubts, conflicts, counter-suggestions, afterthoughts, subthoughts, all budding and proliferating into a vegetable image, not exactly a tree but at first a spiky century plant putting up a rod of blooms like Brussels sprouts and then, as the dominance of color veered from the warm purples to bluish greens, a wrinkling and complication of the spikes into banks of menacing coral from which immense waving forests of kelp and seagrape and sea-lettuce sprang up, in delicate but rather cold shades of turquoise, aquamarine. The music now was Hindemith, Bloch. For the first time, as this endlessly subdividing complexity of his idealism was borne in upon John, he felt ever so slightly oppressed.

He decided to open his eyes.

Light flooded John's soul. When he was able to bear the thought of looking *at* something, his gaze fell on the op-art print of candy canes, and this was bad luck. The spirals of color began to revolve with dizzying speed, and the canes all seemed to melt and wobble, and when John tore his eyes from the picture, a large section of blank wall at once became an op-art dance of spiral dervishes. Worse, the wall itself was undulating, to music, if it could be called that, electronic howls and clankings, at any rate, by Babbitt, Ussachevsky.

He thought of the lovely rod of glowing purples between the curtain and the sky, and he turned to look at it, to anchor himself on that straight godly glow. To his alarm the line had turned into a dirty green, which jumped with sheer inappropriateness between the red and blue, and like everything else in the room it was unstable, wavy, insubstantial, reptilian.

Now John realized something else. All the furniture in the room, every wavering object, was big, and he was very small. Experiences! He had been through this decades ago, this feeling of being so small, so utterly helpless, so dependent. Would the sphincters hold? Could he keep from bawling? Was his thumb a whirling candy cane?

He had a conviction that now in his renewed infancy he was hearing colors, smelling music, and this filled him with the queerest combination of joy and fear, which honked on and off as everything else in the room pulsated, a meld of delight and panic which made the panic glorious and the delight horrible.

Dimly he thought, to a fantasia of shapes that were like mountains forming, falling, growing, collapsing, that Breed had said something about being afraid. With an exertion of will that strained his every capacity he told himself: Everything is illusion. My senses are taking things from out there and converting them, twisting them, remaking them. It's all right. It will be over by midnight.

He forced his eyes to the clock, and now what delight there had been vanished; nothing left but fright. The face of the clock had begun to melt and was breathing. Living Dali! He had an impulse to laugh at that thought, but the sensation in his throat was of choking. He could not make out the hour and minute hands at all. The second hand was visible, all too visible—a glowing rod of gloomy greens. With much writhing, it was just barely turning. At this rate, thought John, experiencing a tingling and numbness in his hands and feet, midnight would not come for fifty years.

Everything that had happened since he had opened his eyes had been so bad that John thought he would take sanctuary behind the skin of his lids again. But now the inner view was chaotic. Poisonous greens were in charge. An enormous Jackson Pollock confusion of dots, spills, and splotches filled his mind's eye—but alive, splashing, agitated, breathing. It felt as if every one of the ten billion cells of his brain was trying to get attention, to proclaim its special function. There was, now, in all this exploding unreality, only one unity—the burning smell; and beneath the smell, one persistent thread of thought, a kind of endless skreek:

—— It's brimstone. It will always be there. Infinity.

John needed Breed's help. He was going to stand up and walk through a wall.

With the greatest of difficulty he opened his eyes, and he saw Breed's face quite close to his, and he wished he did not.

Breed's skin had gone puce. His cheeks and chin seemed to have the consistency of yoghurt. His eyes— pinwheels. His hair and eyebrows were alive, each dark filament enormously magnified and wriggling. The putty lips moved, and to wobbles of color John heard:

—— Ong ee ay.

Don't be afraid? Was that what this frightful inhuman face had tried to say? Had Breed lost the power of speech? What was the matter with Breed? Breed! Breed! You can't just melt! You have to help me! Stop this! It's too much for me! Help me!

John was terrified lest he, John, might dissolve like the clock face, like Breed's face, like the whole face of reality.

There was a metallic taste on his tongue. His hands and feet felt frozen. He was suffocating.

He tried to cry out: —— Heaven isn't worth Hell!

The paste that had been Breed came closer. It said something:

—— A-a-ah. A-a-ah.

Then John saw the loathly worm. It came down off the opposite wall. It gathered its hump of mobile green segments and then stretched out toward what little was left of the self. John wriggled out of John and watched John and the worm. Then John saw that the worm and John were one and the same, so he went back into him-it.

He-worm hardened into some kind of limestone shape and it-John hung on the lip of a crag at the edge of the sea. Infinity.

26

HE tried to move. He ached. Struggling up slowly from a stone sleep on stone, he arrived first at an awareness of being hot; burning, burning—his chest, his arms, his soul. Milton's hell? The lids of his eyes, on fire, barely screened out a fiery light; he dared not lift them for fear of being blinded.

Now, more awake, he felt the roughness of the rock on which he lay. And he heard ocean sounds—the roar of combers breaking somewhere.

Careful to squint, he opened his eyes and saw the sea: a tropical sea, shifting lights of pale aquamarine over white sand, the froth of combers on coral reefs, and ripe-plum deeps beyond. Good sky-curtain colors, moving as water moves.

Now he remembered, or began to remember. Fragments. How soundly he must have slept! He had stretched out on the rock to sunbathe and had thought to take a nap. Yes. Now. The beach colony. He turned his head and saw the long crescent of sand, the grove of coconut palms in the lee of the gigantic heap of volcanic rocks marking the upper end of the beach, the crude lean-tos of palm fronds the crumb-seekers had built.

The sun was beginning, from a quarter of the way down the sky, its big slow plunge down to the western rim, and the onshore breeze was dying out. Time to rouse himself; he had slept too long. It would soon be time to go up to the resort for the evening's begging.

He was so stiff! What folly to sleep on a rock. His skin tingled. He was hot to the very center of himself.

Groaning, he sat up. He stretched his arms and back and then arose and eased himself down off the huge brown rock onto the sand, and he walked up the beach to the cluster of lean-tos. There was a smell of coffee boiling near Breed's lean-to; that man knew how to live. He saw that most of the colony, about thirty, were drifting up from the beach. In the group coming up from the water there was, as usual, quite a cluster of guys around Laetitia, a runaway girl from Boston whose only talent in life was swimming topless. She used sawed-off jeans for trunks, with wet threads hanging down from the torn edges on her legs like pale seaweed.

Still drowsy, still burning, he crawled into the cool shade of his lean-to and lay down on his sleeping bag, and he began thinking of the joys of being unencumbered— the fierce delight that one could take in begging, which, as Breed had pointed out, was the most primitive of protests. Begging was a form of punishment of those who had wherewithal to give. How rich the faces of the victims!—hating to part with their pennies, guilty, fearful of contamination, yet feeling the power of the giver, condescending, not wanting to encourage bad habits! So funny; so cruel. Yet this was not mere begging; it was crumb-seeking, in good sixteenth-century style. The kids cruised in units—there were six in John's—and they performed before they begged; they put a levy on the haves for being entertained. But even the entertainment could have a double edge, could be partly a mockery, so that the point of this existence was not simply to mount a pure mendicant protest; it was more than that—it was to make a cool existential statement about the absurdity of The Rat Race. That mockery was the part Susan loved, who shared his lean-to. She loved to jive the gringos. She was probably coming up from the beach now.

Gazing out under the lip of the shelter at the softly rattling fingers of palm overhead, he heard a passing couple say:

—— You know something? This might be Easter Sunday.

—— That's a great thought.

—— I've lost track.

—— Frank'll know. He puts notches in his crutch.

—— Isn't that like a crip for you?

Frank was a junior at Michigan State who had severed a hamstring in a motorcycle accident and when walking propped his powerful frame on one old-fashioned wooden crutch. He was the third man in John and Breed's unit, and he was in a sense the indispensable one. Besides having a sunburst of a red beard and a passable deep singing voice, he had as well a true genius—for passing the hat. He was the best of beggars: a pleasing cripple. The rich Hispanos always kicked in big for him, and the effect he produced on the North American tourists was electrifying: they gave him only rebukes. A fine young man like him doing that!

Here came Susan, itching to leave.

—— Isn't it nearly time to go?

Susan was a big-boned girl who did folksongs in what Breed called a Mount Holyoke-choirgirl-Baez style. Her long hair was parted in the middle and hung down straight. She was obsessed with keeping her guitar dry, and now she took it out to bake it a few minutes in the late-afternoon sunlight. From beyond the lean-to she asked John:

—— What'll I wear tonight? (She had only one outfit.)

John: —— Better wear your red blue jeans and your high-heel sneakers.

Susan: —— Yikhhh.

Overhead the palm trees had stopped rattling. The air was still. John was cooler now, but the skin on the front of his body glowed and felt tight. He got up to shuck his bathing trunks and dress. Across the way he heard Breed barking orders at Fay, his girl; he had conned her into climbing a slanting palm tree to get him a good coconut for his breakfast the next morning. Her name was Fay Dillington, Junior, and she was the daughter of a famous designer (female) of shotguns for sportswomen. Here at the encampment Fay was wispy, haggard, and pathetic, for she was nothing more than Breed's servant girl (she reminded John of shadowy Lena in *Victory*), but in the evenings she was something else again, coming on after Susan's songs with a stupendous act of making faces.

Breed's voice: —— Not that one! No, *no!* Reach down under there. That's the one. Work that one loose. Come on, Fay, snap into it.

Just then Susan whanged out on her guitar the wild annunciatory chords of a flamenco dance and shouted:

—— Come on, team! Time to go.

Quite promptly Frank's red bush of a mug came rocking above his three-point limp from behind the massive lean-to he had built; he was in drooping rust-red shorts that clashed in color with his beard, and a not-too-clean T-shirt. Laetitia was his girl, and she followed him, expressionless but willing, in her swimming jeans, still damp, and a Beethoven sweatshirt. After coming up from the beach and covering herself, Laetitia could do nothing but stand around; Frank even had to fix their meals. In the evenings she had a certain value just gooping with her mouth open, because she looked so homeless. The only money North Americans ever put in the hat was because of how forlorn she looked (if only they could have seen her in the afternoons). The unit had tried letting her shake a pair of gourds with dried beans in them, but she hadn't been able to keep time.

Frank, with his monotonous two-hundred-pounder's cheerfulness: —— Where to, tonight?

Susan: —— Pretty please, the Tanampa.

But Breed, who never missed a thing, apparently had a different idea; he called from his lean-to, suggesting one of the new places on the cliffs above the resort, called La Playa Courts. Susan shouted arguments to Breed, and he finally conceded that they might end up the evening at the Tanampa. At that Susan jumped and clapped her hands; but she was too heavy to play baby.

Now Breed and Fay approached, and John, having shaken the sand out of his sleeping bag and having tossed the bag back under the lean-to, looked up at them and vividly saw, in the slanting sunlight, why the tourists reacted so violently to the sight of this couple. They were dressed identically in outfits both of which belonged to Breed: long slacks, once crisp yellow linen, now wrinkled and filthy, with the cuffs turned up to just below the knees, and moldy long-sleeved Basque shirts with horizontal blue stripes. But the real shock was their hair—identical mops, Breed's even longer than he usually wore it at school, Fay's precisely like his. They seemed interchangeable persons who must, one thought at first glance, have had interchangeable parts—the idle hermaphroditic joke of that winter, which for some reason gave the older generation total gut-shudders.

Off they all went toward the resort on a donkey-cart track, six pairs of bare feet shuffling through the dust to atone for having been scrubbed clean in the surf during the day. As they went over the first rise John looked back at the incredible beauty of an untouched place. There were no signs of human life to be seen besides the cluster of lean-tos; there was no paved road out this way from the resort; the nearest settlement was a clutch of Indio fishermen's huts on a cove sheltered by an island beyond the next point. Everyone in the beach colony kept saying how lucky they were—there weren't many clean spots left in the sun, this place would be spoiled by next year, there'd be three thousand impossible rah-rah types with surfboards camping on the beach, going in for a lot of cruddy beer-hounding and tail-sniffing and, finally, rioting.

The track wound over barren ridges and ducked down into dark forests in the hollows between; coming back to the encampment through these low places at night, with nothing to show the way but Breed's pen-sized flashlight, gave the girls quite a thrill.

Three miles is a good bracing walk. Frank, who was very strong in spite of his bad leg, or because of it, became exuberant and hopped, half ran, and vaulted on his crutch. Susan would not let anyone relieve her of her guitar, safe from the sea air in its case; she swung along like a Marine.

John liked her. There was a blandness about her, a lack of imagination, but she was a rackety, flat-out, no-hidden-places girl. Her sex was like her folksongs: melancholy, faked-up, so muted and understated as to be not quite there at all. Old experienced John had had the pleasant feeling that he was taking her in hand, giving her some know-how. However, sleeping bags were not all they were cracked up to be as beds of roses; someone was always getting a foot caught, and when such a thing happened Susan had a disconcerting habit of laughing loud and hard.

They stood on a high finger of land, where they could see the resort in full view ahead, and they looked out to watch the sun dive into the calm sea, with a flashing crown of brilliant green as the last small elastic cap of its unbearable light finally went under. Then they walked on.

The edge of town was abrupt. The donkey-cart track stopped; asphalt paving started. Villas, privacy, walls. Off to the right they could see, from time to time, the famous bay. The tower of the Felicidad-Hilton loomed at its far end, a flamingo-pink testimony to man's ultimate contempt for nature's gifts. Back of the town, and above it on rocky crests, were several of the new tourist traps, with big glass views, blue swimming pools, and bars with fanny-shaped plastic chairs on mushroom bases.

The unit headed for the plaza, the center of the old town, halfway along the curve of the bay. In the middle of the old square were nice smelly open market sheds, where it was fun in daytime to steal vegetables. Among other buildings on the plaza were a stuccoed church, a number of provision shops, and the original hotel, El Mirador, with colonnades and porches, tall windows that were shuttered at midday, and big lazy wooden-bladed electric fans in every public room. El Mirador obviously had the only good food in the resort, but North American tourists never went to the place; too many flies, they said, no air conditioning. Near it, doubtless the despair of the genteel Hispanos who stayed there, was a noisy native dive called the Tanampa, which was so lowdown as to be considered ultra-chic by North Americans who had the most money—enough money to really get away, as John's mother might have put it.

Breed had said they could wind up at the Tanampa late that night; John, feeling the glow of sunburn all down his front, dimly felt he should husband his powers for that last hour. The reason Susan loved the Tanampa was that the management there let units get right out on the dance floor to perform; at the fancy places you had to cringe around the outskirts waiting for an opening, or sidle up to a table and just have the brass to start in.

The beach side of the plaza was a palmetto-lined promenade, and kids from the colony had from the beginning taken over one corner of it, at the south end. Natives never came near that corner, now. It was, for the young North Americans, a safe spot to wait for the tourists to get drunk, a place to gather anger. Boys from other units left their girls and crowded around Laetitia, who at this hour had nothing to offer them but the wild-haired deaf German genius on her front—and memories. Frank became sullen. Susan got her guitar out and strummed softly a long time, and later she and John sang "Aura Lee": *Sunshine came along with thee, and swallows in the air.* There was a tautness in their voices, expectancy.

At last the units began to drift off. Breed led the way up to the crags behind the town. As they climbed, John fell into a strange, hazy frame of mind, in which he felt more potential than actual. The next two or three hours were rather blurred in his mind. He dimly sensed that La Playa Courts, a motel that might as well have been in Florida, turned out to be a bust, half empty and cold, with a strong smell of fresh paint, and Susan and Fay were furious with Breed, and Breed laughed at their anger; and they went down and performed at the side-walk tables in front of El Mirador and on the porches over the street colonnade, and when the dining room closed they went around to the back door and sang, and one of the cooks brought out a big iron tureen with the remains of that day's *gazpacho,* and they sat in the dusty street with dogs and goats around them and dipped out the cold sharp stuff with their bare hands.

Just after midnight they eased into the Tanampa, and John became alert.

The place was crammed—a choice crop of sozzled Norteamericanos, and a large number, too, of rather tough-looking natives. Five bedraggled peasants, with two guitars and a trumpet, were singing a funny-sad song called *El hijo desobediente,* about a bad son. To legitimize themselves, John's unit stood at the bar and bought, out of their collections, three Carta Blancas to share.

John's attention was drawn at once to a party of six at a table on the edge of the tiny dance floor, and particularly to a woman in that group, an old girl of about fifty, wearing a silk print dress, pearls, white shoes, carrying a native woven-reed handbag—absolutely standard stuff; yet there was something peculiarly inviting about her. She must have been beautiful once. Her gestures were unaffectedly feminine, her sad eyes were set in deep hollows; she looked as if she had both a flirtatious vulnerability and an unusual aptitude for disapproval. *She was just right.*

The *paisanos* subsided with one last sagging run of the trumpet. There was a lull. Susan said:

—— Come on, kids. The zero hour.

Then they were out on the floor peddling their wares. At first everything went in a routine way. From the beginning John stared at Mrs. Silk Print. He saw her notice it; she shifted in her chair, crossed her legs. John knew that he looked ghoulish—on his chin was not a beard but simply ten days' negligence—but he caught her giving him a sickly smile, and he knew she was inwardly commiserating with that poor boy's parents back home, while at the same time she wanted to stroke his forehead, tell him a bedtime story.

While Susan sang her songs, Frank's deep voice mimicked a string bass, now bowed, now plucked, zum zoom batoobatoob toob toob, producing, beneath Susan's first song, a very funny effect of musical skepticism of a lament for lost virginity she was voicing. She sang next the woes of an Emily Dickinson-type shut-in, parting starched curtains to peer out at the world. Then Fay did her grimacing act. John saw incredulity and disgust blooming on Mrs. Silk Print's face.

Then Breed and John did a thing of singing college songs in harmony, holding their noses as they sang. The natives, who probably couldn't understand Word One, seemed to lose their minds over a musically non-sequiturish medley Breed and John sang that way, of isolated lines from Middle-Western college songs, such as *Shake down the thunder from the sky* (Notre Dame), *Never daunted, you shall not falter* (Indiana), *Sing to the colors that float in the night* (Michigan), *We'll back your stand, you're the best in the land* (Illinois). There must have been some Yanqui-Wants-to-Go-Home feeling in those nasal twangs. Madam Print's eyes burned with indignation.

Frank passed the hat, and the take from the natives was good. John, shivering now in a fever of sunburn and hot scorn, kept his eyes on the North American woman.

Suddenly he felt as if he were climbing the face of an old wooden tenement building.

He stepped out in front of the group and began a wild patter in triple-talk—in bogus Spanish, French, and English. The non-words simply flew off his lips. The whole time he leered at Madam Print, who had begun to have the weirdest look on her hollow-eyed face, of censure, lust, patriotism, hatred, and need for help. John was speaking with tongues; peeping through the brilliant glossolalia were a whole series of subliminal flashes, never explicit, never even whole words, of not-quite-decent suggestions. The natives had begun to laugh and clap; two other units of kids moved out from the bar and started to shout things like *olé!* and up-John! and sock-it-to-'er! The woman was blushing and grinning a perfectly awful grin.

Now came the flood of feelings shooting every which way, and suddenly John sprang forward, bent down over the woman, twisted his body into a satyr's lustful stance, and loudly asked:

—— Why do you look like a monkey?

Involuntarily Mrs. Print turned around to the others in her group, evidently for a gulp of moral superiority.

John went on as her face turned back to his:

—— Gibbon a ringtail rangtang orilla-la mandrill orilla-la bluebottom chimpozee Jesus-rhesus—

She cried out: —— You call yourself an American!

—— We're all Americans here (an arm sweeping over Latin Americans and Norteamericanos alike).

She realized her mistake, which she must have been making forty times a day, and she spat out: —— You know what I mean, kiddo.

John now cried out in triumph: —— You're drunk-o Mrs. Monkey-o.

She stood up and stuck her face out toward John's. He pushed his a bit closer to hers.

She: —— If you must know, I've had exactly two tequilas. I never take more than two cocktails. Ever.

—— Two is one too many, dear.

She was weeping now, and John, seeing spider-web wrinkles on her cheeks, realized, as his skin burned hotter than ever, that it was not simply tourists he despised, not these certain representatives of a certain way of life—it was, rather, a generation; it was the *age* of the woman that infuriated him. He was young, young, young, and he felt a wild sunburned joy in his youthfulness. The thought of decay was loathesome; he hated the older spics just as much as the older tourists.

The woman: —— You should be *ashamed*. You degenerate! You stand there full of marijuana or something and accuse me—

—— A person doesn't eat marijuana, you can't get full of it. You bre-e-e-eathe it.

—— Legett. Legett! (Now she appeared to have become terrified, both of John and of herself.) Do something. Get the Consul down here and do something about these . . . these beatniks.

John stretched out his arms and said: —— How about let's go out on the beach and let me hump you?

She gasped as if John had thrown a glass of cold beer in her face.

—— Legett!

One of the men, evidently the selfsame Legett, leaned back in his chair and said: —— Attagirl, Janey. You give it to him plenty!

The place was suddenly in an uproar. One of the other units, with two guitars, unable to contain itself, broke into a crummy rock-'n'-roll number, and John began to do the Swim in a not-nice way close to Mrs. Print. The older natives, sensing that some tide had turned against them, too, had begun to mutter, whistle, thump on tables.

John thought he would burst with emotion. He wanted to weep with pity for the woman, and for himself; to laugh his head off; to thumb his nose at the woman's tight husband, at the old spics, at the older everyone; to spit at the woman; but to respond also to the lasciviousness he saw in her deep eye sockets—and to flee, for now he saw two dark-skinned men get up from a table at the side of the floor and start toward him.

Out of the side of his eye he saw crippled Frank clopping sidewise on enormous crutch-jumps, saw him bump each of the men hard with his off-crutch shoulder, and swerve left. This gave the unit time to run.

27

AGAIN his sleep had a density, like that of a viscous liquid, and rising from it required an effort, a kind of swim. He felt, indeed, damp—face, hands, soul. He wanted to see the day, if there was a day yet. One eye fluttered open; the other seemed to be stuck shut with sleep-paste, a thickened mucus. The open eye saw a thorough silence of fog—pre-dawn grayness, thickness, a bisque of nowhere. He brought a hand up to rub the glued lid open, and the knuckles hit a hard edge. Of course. His helmet shell.

He was so sore! He closed his eyes to run off an inventory of his discomforts. He was lying on his back, the bad-dream position. Head held stiffly in place by the webbing of the shell; feet like clubs, confined all night in those ungiving boots; a rock against a kidney. Once in the

night, stirring in pain, he had laughed, thinking: —— My
kidney stone's bugging me.

Eyes still closed, he lifted his right arm and groped
with his hand on the lip of the hole. They were there. His
shovel. His rifle. He dropped the arm.

He must have dug a rotten hole. They kept saying
that the hole you lay down in meant your life. But his
arms must have been heavy the night before, his back
sore, and he must have struck sparks from that rock at
kidney position, and it must have proved too big to pry
out, and he must not have felt like starting all over again.
He couldn't yank up a single clear memory yet.

All the same, he had the impression that he had
slept, when he had slept, as if he himself were an outcropping of the same rock. He felt logy-bodied and light-
headed now. He opened his eyes again and saw the vague
fog again. Raising his head with excruciating concentra-
tion, he made out that he was on a raised place of some
sort, a knee of a grassy ridge, and that indefinite dark
shapes which were probably treetops loomed in the mist
at a somewhat lower level, ahead.

Now. Something about an outpost. And yes. The
squad made a fragmentary arc of a perimeter on the outer
edge of the hill, a thin line dug in just below the cap of
the ridge. They were sleeping in their shallow holes:
Breed, Wagner, Ackercocke, Lusk, Spinter, Faglio, Flack.
And the sergeant: Panzer.

Oh yes my God they were to go out today on a
search-and-destroy mission. The squad's first trial. Panzer, a potato-waist of a regular who had been in Korea
and who kept grousing in reverse, telling everybody how
much better conditions were here than there, had called
this mission that had been assigned to them an exercise,
as if they were going down to the Y for a workout, where

the worst hazards would be a mild case of jock itch or the foot. Panzer and his Korean terrors: blinding snowstorms and waves of gooks.

It was lighter now. John heard voices along the line. He tried to turn onto his right side, but his body was a rigid sculpture of bones and wires.

Here came the sergeant, up-an'-at-'em, storming along below the skyline, routing people out with endless abusive roaring:

—— Up, up, heave ass, you phonies, you fake sojers. . . .

John managed to reach a sitting position. The fog now seemed to be a steam rising from the hollow below the ridge. What was simmering down there? Search whom and destroy what? Gristle-sore, famished, dizzied by sitting up, John had the most unsettling feeling of dissociation. Who was the enemy? Who were the guerrillas roaming in bands in the miasma down there? Hispanos?

Slantheads? Greasers? Rednecks? Minutemen? Hoods from downtown? Guys from Garrison, Sheldon's rival college?

How horrible not to be able to remember who the enemy was!

John leaned forward and put his face in his hands. He felt that he would be brave, later in the day, in the idiotic sense that he would be willing to die—but that was only because, as it happened, he was not unwilling to die. What tightened his stomach muscles and prolonged his giddiness now was that he had no idea what he was being asked to be willing to die for. One thing certain: No one ever saw this enemy. Panzer kept saying that *out there*, meaning in Korea, you could see millions of Chinks coming at you—whereas here, silence; invisible guerrillas. John supposed he could draw on an inner fund of patriotism, because really one was lucky to be able to live in a house with a glass wall on the edge of Worcester. And surely there was reality in the phrase consent of the governed (except that here was Dom Faglio, three holes down, to remind one of the Negroes in Mississippi). Search and destroy. The concept seemed so negative. Indeed the whole mood of this setting was negative: fear of them, fear of *their* designs on *us*, fear of what the guerrillas would do to the good guys.

John heard Breed calling out: —— Hey, Sarge, can we for Godsakes light a fire and brew up some coffee?

Panzer's roar was of a soul being tried in boiling oil: —— Fire, my ass! Where you think you're at, Breed? The Muelbach Hotel? You want room service? FIRES MAKE SMOKE!

Breed's voice was conversational: —— Sergeant Panzer, I have to report I can't eat this crap without coffee. I'll be *hors de combat* later in the day.

Panzer: —— What a generation of so-called tiger men! Look, Breed. *Out there* they given you one choice only, you ate it or you din eat. Look, Christ, here you got your choice of Pard, Ken-L-Ration, Alpo, Pal, Gainesburgers. What more you want?

Breed: —— Coffee.

Then it was Ackercocke: —— Hey, Sarge, is it true the major's going out with us today?

Panzer: —— He's liable. I haven't heard definite, but I don't put it past the son of a bitch.

Ackercocke: —— Isn't it unusual for a major to go out on search-and-destroy with a lousy little platoon?

Panzer: —— Look, Aching Cock, this major ain't usual no ways. He may look like a perfessor to you motherfugging pen-pushers, but let me tell you one thing: he's got a pair of balls like they're stainless steel. Where he goes, baby, I go. So. Do. You.

John took off his shoes and rubbed his feet and wiggled his toes awhile. Breed called a greeting from the next hole, too chillingly calm. John opened a ration box and tried to force down some dehydrated concentrates. It started to rain, to groans and curses all along the ridge. John put his poncho over his head and stood up.

As he straightened up, dizziness and disorientation assaulted him. His head began to spin, he saw the whirling candy canes on the wavering wall of Breed's room, he felt as if he were clutching a porch pillar for dear life. It occurred to him that what he had swallowed a few minutes before had been a concentrate of time; dehydrated chronology. He hung on. He half expected to hear Susan, in mad disregard of the drizzle, strumming folk stuff.

Instead he heard Sergeant Panzer's roar: —— Awright, awright, all you little flits get over here. Come on, you dandy citizen-sojers. Double-ass time!

Then John turned and saw the major approaching from the crest, and he was filled with panic.

Major Malcolm Fist. It was his father.

His first coherent thought, while the fear still hummed through him: —— All that guff about starched white uniforms.

The men of Panzer's squad and those of the next squad around the bend of the ridge—together, First Platoon, Company C—assembled around the sergeant's foxhole, which, with its finicky squared corners and its depth of a potter's-field grave, should have been lifted right out of wherever this was and been shipped for posterity's wonderment to the Smithsonian in Washington.

John hung back at the outer rim of the half circle of dogfaces. He felt that his father could have looked at him but deliberately did not. Unlike the rest of the men, his father had shaved. In the shadow of his steel helmet his face looked molded out of fog material; grim and drawn. He was wearing a camouflage poncho. A yellow leaf was painted on his helmet. *Acer saccharum?* Golden leaves in October.

When the major spoke, John trembled, and his hands felt clammy—that ineffectual voice!

—— All right, fellows, let's move over here away from this . . . this mine shaft of Sergeant Panzer's. Gather round. Close up. I want you to be able to see this map of mine.

He had gone down on one knee and was unfolding to the gentle drizzle a topographical map, with amoebic contour lines, and blues, greens, and yellows of various altitudes. John took one look and saw the protozoan lines begin to stretch, as if the hills were putting out pseudo-pods to ooze and move and beget by division; he could not bear the sight and looked away. The men crowded around, crouching in front, others leaning forward.

—— Now listen and watch closely. We'll go down off the ridge into this draw here. Single file as we go down. Keep five paces. I'll take the point and then I want two good men, Sarge, to be my flankers later. Who've you got?

John, even though he was at the back of the group, bent his knees and lowered his head, in order not to be seen, not to be named at any cost.

—— This buncha lily-livers, I ain't got much, Major, I'm telling you. . . . O.K. Wagner. Who the hell else? . . . All right. Faglio the *vaglio.*

Some of the men laughed, whether at Faglio or in simple relief, it would have been hard to say. John found himself coughing.

—— Then you next, Sergeant. Then squads as usual. Keep spread out, everyone. Now, when we reach the stream, we'll fill our canteens and for heaven's sakes don't forget to put in your anti-trots pills. We'll cross over wherever we can find a ford and then we'll spread out in a search line. I'll be front center with my flankers. Keep about ten paces. . . .

John wasn't looking at the map, for fear its shapes would oscillate, creep, pucker; and he wasn't really listening any more. His father's voice seemed to be becoming old Orreman's voice, half cracked, self-loving, with a resonance now of the big fights—the goose flight of lateen sails down the purple sound at Salamis; the few brave men at the pass; *and the swift bronze spearhead drove through the sevenfold-oxhide shield* . . . John felt the terror of the failing mark arching like a shafted weapon, long-shadowed, through the air at him.

—— We'll pause there to wait for the air show. The support will be saturation, they've promised some really big bangs followed by a good thorough napalming. Weather permitting.

His father's eyelids flapped upward and his eyes seemed to search the rim of his helmet for a sight of the godhead parting the clouds with hands that were themselves made of clouds. A look of distaste. A shudder? John felt sick at his stomach; the time capsule he had swallowed was curdling, and he might throw up bile-tinted weeks, months, years, entire developmental spans. Was his father *afraid*?

—— We think their bivouac is in that tuck in the hills there.

And so they started down the draw to search for something that someone thought was somewhere.

John hung back and cut into the line about halfway

to the rear. The first descent was down a steep ravine into a forest of huge trees. It was dark in the draw. The drizzle stopped, and between the great boles big drops fell from time to time from the moisture-catching heads of the trees. On the forest floor, in a transept light, were many leggy plants, some bearing pale flowers. Toadstools grew in the leaf mold.

Silence, but for equipment clicking, shoes squoosh-ing. The men put their feet down carefully—could they all have been onetime readers of James Fenimore Cooper? *Kra-a-a-a!* A bird scream. All down the line men threw up forearms to protect their helmeted heads.

The front of the line came to a creek. Canteen-filling took forever and ever, world without end. At last John reached the stream; the water was muddy, but he filled up and dropped in a pellet that he took from his cigarette-pack pouch, an unrolled condom tied upon itself.

He waded across the stream, getting wet to his thighs, and took his place in the search line, and found that by chance, because of where he had cut into the file on the way down, he was now aligned with the point—not thirty feet behind the major. At this discovery he expected a new onset of panic. Instead, he began to be calm, he felt protected—and angry.

On a hand signal from the major the line started forward. It raked the forest for about half a mile, moving onto gradually rising terrain. Then the major turned and raised both arms. The line halted.

A long wait for air support.

Would the planes get through the low clouds? Would they find the right target if they did?

John's father never even looked at him. John began really to burn: —— Who does he think he is?

Then, zowie, the flutter of a marker copter, the small

thud of a smoke bomb. A roar of jets came on, and very soon, dead ahead, obviously dead on the target, dead was the word, the silence of the forest was shattered by the god-damnedest thunderation John had ever heard. It had never been remotely like this on the boob tube: those war-nostalgia specials, Winston Churchill and Iwo Jima and all. All that dubbed-in kettledrumming had never re-motely suggested this. The living-room floor had never shaken like this ground, the curtains had never fluttered in the shock waves as the leaves above now did, dropping sudden sheets of water.

John thought of the guerrillas in their bivouac. His little anger fed on every earthshake, and he soon felt a towering fury at his father.

The explosions were quickly ended. A second whoosh of jets could be heard, and a series of lesser thumps, and then a steady roar and crackling. And up the further rise through the tall trunks John could see the walls of Hell, curling and boiling like the underlip of a line squall, brilliant orange and vest red, with a Gorgon-head of writhing black smoke-curls. John, thinking of the pale cuplike flowers, the toadstools, the guerrillas, felt ghastly heat, outer and inner, on the skin of his cheeks.

In time the bomb-fire spent itself, and John could hear a shocking steady sea-sound—the hissing of the rain on the hot ashes. The blackened slope began to steam.

All the while they waited for the hillside to cool, John was thinking: —— It's *his* fault. You always heard people say what a pleasant, agreeable man he was. If only they knew! Values! In the mouth.

An arm wave. They went forward. Soon they were in the blackened, ruined temple. The trees were bare, the trunks charred. Where was the bivouac, where the zillion corpses strewn around that John dreaded? The line was halfway through the burnt-out place. John's legs up to his knees were covered with black ashes.

Then came Wagner's triumphant roar: —— Here it is! I've found it!

The line broke. Curiosity gathered the men. Wagner had found the so-called bivouac—a little stone fireplace, a frying pan. It appeared that a lone man had been fixing his breakfast. In the half-melted frying pan lay the crisp remains, the carbonized shape, showing some of the skeleton, of a fish that the man had apparently been frying. Had he caught it in a forest stream?

They looked for the body. It was nowhere.

They turned back, to return to base in single file. Now Sergeant Panzer was at the head of the line. John looked around; his father was next behind him in the line, but John, surprised again, could not be angry. Everything struck him as funny. Until.

Not long after the first of the line re-entered the green forest a single sharp crack could be heard ahead. The line abruptly halted. After a long wait a whispered message came back. Flack, ahead of John, stepped to him and whispered in his ear. John turned and walked to his father and whispered up under the rim of the helmet:

—— They got Panzer.

Oh, the rich comedy (overdrawn shame, guilt, frustration, fear of loss of face) under the proscenium of the helmet with the maple leaf, the instant Aristophanes, the Molière, the Wycherley, the Shaw, the Kaufman, all the ages of the belly laugh! Quick rundown of all-time farce, only the best. Rich, rich.

Another crack from another quarter. Was it just the one man, his breakfastless gut griping him as he moved around in the forest?

Then John's father murmured to John: —— Come with me. I need you.

That ended the laughing part. John and the major went to the top of the line. They moved again. Four men carried Panzer's chunky body. Lusk had been hit in the shoulder; he could walk with support.

Now utterly exposed, here at the point, John was astonished—horrified, really—to see the major's integrity. He could see from his father's demeanor, from his walk when they moved, from the way he gave orders when another rifle shot cut the air, from his face when he spoke to his son, from his response to the news that a second man had been killed, that he was not afraid of death. But that he was also nuts about being alive. He was unshakably solid. John felt a tremor in his hands.

A third good guy was killed. A fourth. Search and destroy indeed! They moved along the forest floor, pausing when a shot cracked, passing the word to keep thinned out. The trembling in John's hands worsened.

They were moving again. John's eyes roved through the noble woods. There! Ten feet off the ground. In the crotch of a twin-trunked giant—was it a species of beech? *Fagus grandifolia?* In the vee, a roundness. A burl? No! Surely a helmetless head; surely the sniper himself. Word came forward to hold up a minute, the bearers were having it rough. The men stood in fear. John, saying nothing, stared at the tree crotch. Now he felt the familiar onrush of feelings, the flood of everything at once, in every direction. With unprecedented force. He spoke to his father:

—— The whole operation is ridiculous.

—— We can't help that, son. It's out of our hands.

—— Is it really? I mean, that idea gives me a real pain in the ass. Aren't you in charge?

—— Keep your shirt on, fellow.

As they talked John felt that he was maneuvering his father. There were some slender saplings between where they stood and the tree crotch where the round shape was. Stepping aside little by little, keeping the talk going so that his father, too, inched sidewise to catch the murmured words, John constantly faced the tree crotch; his father's body, shielding his own, was placed with its back exposed to the double tree.

Now they were in the open. John, his heart on the run, suddenly became convinced that the odd shape was, after all, a queer growth, a burl, perhaps a paper-wasp nest.

But then a whine came ridden hard by a snap.

As his father fell, with the faintest sign of reproach on his otherwise empty face, John felt such an exquisite pain in his chest that he thought the bullet must have passed through both generations.

28

A MALE nurse stood by the door in short-sleeved white, his hairy arms swinging to urge the patients to chug along.

John, keeping one hand on his chest, which still hurt, entered, slip-slop, on the straw sandals supplied by the hospital.

The patients were going from the maximum-security wards into the day room for R.T.—recreational therapy; love conquers all. The day room was a large rectangular chamber with high ceilings, furnished with pieces that could not be picked up and thrown, and the sunlight pouring in the tall barred windows did its best to make the room cheerful, but the walls were painted a gray of warships, sleet storms, cellar floors, turned hair.

John was in a "mood"; he did not know whether the patients in the room were really who they seemed to him to be. That woman by the window, resembling the Mona whom John thought he remembered, might indeed be Mona, but she might also be, for words that came from her rosebud mouth suggested she believed herself to be, Helen of Troy. And that white-haired man beside her— was that Mr. Sylvian Orreman of the Classic Ideal? When maybe-Mona became really convincing as maybe-Helen, the old man, at any rate, fell in blissfully with the delusion; made a foul pun—said he was in the Priam of life. Cheerfulness, one gathered, was his incurable illness. But there went a young man in an envelope of unpleasantness, who shuffled over to one of the daybeds at the side of the room and lay down with his face to the wall and did not stir; he looked suspiciously like horrible Flack— could it be he? Was that big guy, moving from group to group, challenging, challenging, till people just had to be rude to him and send him away, Wagner? A woman was sitting forward in a chair with her face in her hands, her shoulders shaking with dry, silent sobs, and John, never having seen Professor Gutwillig's wife, never having known for sure that there *was* a Mrs. Gutwillig, was nevertheless positive that she was Mrs. Gutwillig.

———— Helen (John said to maybe-Helen), you look great.

And did she not. John was vividly precise (yes, this vividness, this startling exactness, this incredible instantaneous availability of trade names and *connections,* was the mystery and bane of John's "mood") as he ticked off her charms, to wit: Her hair hung down loose in the sunlight almost to her hips, its near-black flecked with touches of Clairol red-glints; her eyes were sea-green and amorous, the upper lids a Helena Rubinstein insomniac blue; her mouth was generous, soft, of a Dorothy Gray mid-pink; and her cheeks were round and drawn up in little festoons of self-assured amiability dusted with Revlon Love Pat. She looked here and there with a rolling hawk's eye, with a wanton and inviting glare that was driving the male nurses nuts.

Orreman (to John): —— Ahem. The name again?

There was a flickering moment in which John saw, or thought he saw, the benign old fellow sneaking a sheath knife out of his coat pocket, and there was a sharp impression in his mind that the blade was engraved with the unmentionable fourth letter of the alphabet, which, leaping off the blade toward John, seemed to have a dreadful effulgence, a power to burn the eyes of anyone who looked at it, even from a distance. John decided to be very careful, and he said:

—— No name. Anomie. Ego-loss.

—— Never mind (the old man said). We were talking about how to end the war.

Mona-Helen: —— You have to reach the outgoing, loving side of human beings. It's up to the women. Women make babies.

Orreman-Priam: —— My theory is this. If the young men would only decide: killing is wrong, killing is the one absolute wrong. And they'd say, no thanks, I'm not having any of it. They would just refuse. You couldn't make them kill. If enough of them decided to abstain, that would be the end of it. Refuse to kill. I mean in very large numbers.

But had they said this at all? John's "mood" was becoming worse.

Wagner came over, if it was Wagner. He wasn't buying the Troy jazz.

—— Sure, sure (he said), her face is O.K., she's no
dog, but it wasn't the face that launched the ships. Whist!
S-h-h! Listen. She fux. She took on Paris, Hector, Priam.
Then after, Menelaus, Ajax, Odysseus. Even Nestor. Then
after that, the crews. The sailors. A thousand ships.

John: —— Oh, Wagner, hang up. You're disturbed.
You're really tuned up. Look how quiet Flack is.

Wagner: —— Sure, sure, now Metlin T. Flack's the
big model patient.

Then the old man who may have been Orreman
said: —— We have laws against murder to protect society.
Why isn't all killing a crime? You see, it's for the young to
take on their own shoulders. Just say, it's wrong. No,
thanks. Not me. Get someone else. An absolute one-
hundred-percent shutdown on killing by the young.

Mona: —— It's up to the mothers.

The atmosphere in the room was suddenly turned on,
and John's "mood" seemed to dissolve like a morning fog;
he was alert. A doctor, whose name was Flankton, wearing a coat the color of the melancholy walls, a Tattersall
vest, a stiff collar, and a black knit tie, and with a dribble
of food, possibly Cream of Wheat, on his left lapel, so
that he made altogether a fake-European, shabby-natty,
absentminded-genius impression, had entered the room
and was wandering from loon to loon. John was afraid of
him, for he had asked one of the long-time patients what
Dr. Flankton's problem was, and the answer had been:
—— He's a maniac on the subject of shock treatment. A
real monomaniac. He doesn't use shock delicately to help
a patient become reachable as a human being, he uses it
like fire, like hot coals on a grill, like hellfire, forty, fifty,
sixty treatments, to shrivel and shrivel and shrivel the
symptoms. The so-called symptoms. (So the long-time
patient had said.)

In his circling the doctor came eventually to the group around Helen of Troy.

—— How's the most beautiful woman in the world? (He put a hand on Mona's shoulder.)

Mona shrank away, pouting.

—— John? How you doing?

At first John wanted to avoid answering, but the doctor took a step toward him, looking closely at him, as if judging his silence, and John decided it would be safer to answer.

—— My chest hurts.

—— Where?

—— Right here.

—— Don't worry about it. Get your mind off it.

Then John thought he would make light of it, put the doc on, and he said: —— Listen. (He dropped his voice to a whisper.) I think I've got lead poisoning. From a bullet.

—— Really? (Professional humoring, John thought. He's pretending to go along with me.)

—— I ought to be in a regular hospital. Get it cut out.

—— We can take care of it. (An incipient glint in the eye, a pat on the back.) We'll begin some treatments tomorrow. (The doctor's eyebrows twitched downward, his cheeks jumped, and both eyes were pressed tight over that fierce glint by a sudden tic.) We can melt it out.

—— No! No! I was joking, Doctor. Not that! I've heard about you! I don't want that!

Visiting hours began, and Grandma Newson came to see John. They sat at a small square table surfaced with walnut-grained plastic. John's grandmother opened a package of Lorna Doone cookies; the crackling of the wrapper as she tore at it was horrendous, like a huge fire in a forest. She offered John a cookie; he refused, not

217

trusting her. The world's blue-ribbon best-in-breed best-in-show bitch.

—— Your mother sent love.

—— If she loves me so much, why doesn't she come to see me?

—— She's terrified of places like this. You know how hard it would be for her.

—— Listen, Gam, you've got to help me. I want to get out of here. Those male nurses are sadists.

—— You signed yourself in.

—— I know, the whole thing is voluntary. Look, Gam, what kind of an idiot do you take me for? I read that fine print. It said that after five days I had a complete total absolute constitutional moral human right to walk out any time I wanted. Sure, sure. Every door you walk through, click, click, they lock it behind you.

—— Dr. Stampleman up in Worcester says—

—— Look, Gam, you don't seem to understand, something terrible is happening. There's a doctor right here who wants to start frying me on his electric table. He threatened me today. He's crazy, Gam. He said he was going to start tomorrow. They'll get those goons to hold me down. You've got to help me.

—— Let's talk about something a little more pleasant.

—— Brother!

The conversation became more pleasant from John's grandmother's point of view; she talked about the murder of Mrs. Liuzzo, the burglary of the Star of India, the bombing of Zone D by B-52s. Sane topics.

Then after a while, apparently feeling that she had had a soothing effect on John, she left.

Later Chum Breed came to visit. He and John sat in two aluminum-rod chairs near the billiard table, at which

Wagner, chalking and chalking the cue tip after each shot, was putting all of his brutal power into each thrust of the inlaid shaft; the balls cracked like snipers' reports.

John: —— My grandmother was here.

Breed: —— Which side?

—— My mother's. I've told you about her. The bitch one.

—— Ah, yes.

—— I'm scared, Breed. She convinced me I'm really . . . sick.

—— How'd she do that?

—— Look, she's dead. She's been dead eight years.

Breed leaned toward John, and he appeared to be enthralled by John's words.

—— This must be the richest experience of all.

—— Listen, you big shit, you got me into this, now get me out.

Breed was in a rapture: —— The depth of this—

—— This is too much. Do you hear me? This is too much.

—— "The road of excess leads to the palace of wisdom."

—— I mean it, Chum. There's an insane doctor here who wants to destroy me. (O God! Was that what the smell had been all along? Premonition of the mad doctor's brain burner?) He's a shock-therapy nut. He wants to start in on me tomorrow. You've got to help me.

—— I love that about your grandmother.

—— You're not listening to me. Look, Chum, do you know what this place is like? No one *listens* to you here. You try to talk sense, you use words the way you've used them all your life, but they might as well be balls of cotton coming out of your mouth. Words have no value here; they aren't accepted. When the words come out of your mouth, people—and I mean doctors, visitors, the ones they call sane, not just patients—people nod, shake their heads, give you black looks; they react physically to the sounds you make, but you aren't getting through. At first you feel helpless; this collapse of your own words strips you of all humanity, and you begin to get really scared. I guess that's why some of the people around here have taken to just grunting—or going dumb altogether, like animals. But the worst of it is, other people's words reach you. I can hear what old Oval Ears Orreman is saying clearly as a bell, and he sounds to me like the sanest man I know. But I have to assume that he doesn't realize that I receive what he says. *He* doesn't listen to *me*—or anyway doesn't hear me—or anyway doesn't seem to. Everyone here is in a glass container as far as his own utterances are concerned. Words go dead around my own ears as I speak them. I don't feel crazy. The guy named *I* never is. But the catch is, you have to *be* an I, know that you are one, and that's just what's so hard when you lose the power to push your words into other people's heads.

—— Did you have the feeling your words reached people at Sheldon?

—— Different types of nuthouses have different types of accreditation.

—— You mean you think of Sheldon as an asylum, too?

—— This place certifies you as being bughouse; Sheldon certifies you as educated. Both on the basis of the words you use—or rather on the basis of the way they hear, or don't hear, your words. I don't like either deal.

—— What about the other people here? What about that beautiful dame? Can she use words?

—— Mona? She has a non-verbal problem.

—— Interesting? It should be! Whee-oo!

—— Well, no, it's rather common, actually. She's so lovable that she can't find the right man to love her. Why lock her up on that account? She's not going to find him here.

—— What about the problem of safety?

John answered sharply: —— What *about* safety?

—— What about the danger of people hurting themselves? Or hurting others?

—— If you locked up everybody who was potentially dangerous, who would carry the keys?

—— Oh now, John. That *is* a little off base.

John was beginning to talk rather loud: —— I ask you to take wars into account in reckoning who might become dangerous.

—— Wars are a bit special, aren't they? (Breed's teeth glistened in his nicest grin—that of irony.) After all, they're fought for matters of principle.

—— Take into account all the things insurance companies are reluctant to assume any risk for: wars, strikes, riots, civil disturbances, rebellions. They all start with matters of principle. So who's dangerous? The people in here?

—— Don't get excited.

—— I'm *not* excited. (But John knew that he himself now had a hold of a matter of principle and that he was in fact incipiently dangerous.) It's not so-called crazy people who are a threat to others, or to themselves. It's the people who know they're right—who *aren't able to hear anyone else.*

—— You don't have to shout.

—— I'm *not* shouting. (But he was. There was the most provocative, the most infuriating, glint of amusement in Breed's eyes, and a glaze of not hearing, which

made John shout even louder.) What are all these matters of principle anyway? They all come down to one
thing: *Don't stand on my toes.* Hey, you're standing on
my toes. Get off! God damn it, get off my toes!

John was standing up and really sounding off.

He heard Wagner say: —— Look who's disturbed
now.

Breed snapped a thumb and finger in the direction of
the hairy-armed man beside the door. When the nurse
saw Breed's imperious gesture—that of a healthy, well-
adjusted type of person—he turned to the small glass
window in the metal door of the R.T. room (love conquers) and in turn made a signal with his fingers.

John roared at Breed: —— If you don't stand off my
toes I'll bring my free foot into play. I'll kick the bejeezus
out of you.

The door was unlocked from outside and two huge
men entered the room. One was white, the other Negro.
They came toward John, who suddenly began to weep.
To Breed he sobbed:

—— I have a pain in my chest.

Breed, cheer dancing in his eyes: —— What kind?

—— It's a knot of . . . a gob of . . .

—— Breakthrough? Is it a breakthrough?

—— You bastard! You bastard!

The two nurses took hold of John's upper arms, and
the Negro said aside to Breed:

—— This cocky boy won't take his medication. He
puts it in his mouth and tucks it in his cheek and swallows the water. Then later he takes the pill out and puts it
in the cuff of his pants.

The white one said: —— He thinks we don't know it.
There's nothing we don't know.

The Negro, bending down: —— Look.

He turned John's trouser cuff inside out and a dozen round red-and-white pills rolled out on the floor.

The white one: —— Come on, naughty boy.

They danced him along like a marionette, his legs flopping and his feet occasionally knocking on the floor.

John shouted over his shoulder to Breed: —— Get me an I-doctor! Don't turn me over to that kook!

They took John to his room; the white man entered with him, and the metal door clicked behind them. Metal closets flush with a wall; a metal bed with a rough wool blanket; bars in the windows.

—— What're you going to do with me?

—— We're going to take care of you, son.

A vein bulged on the nurse's forehead, emphasizing the ambiguity of that promise.

—— Where's that other one gone?

—— He'll be back.

With a wrench, John got away from the man's grip. They began a chase, ducking, slapping, grabbing, bouncing off walls, jumping over the end of the bed. John, still weeping, also began laughing.

Then the Negro man came in the room with a hypo in his hand. John, eluding his pursuer, lunged at the bare brown arm to try to knock the needle out of the nurse's hand.

They caught him.

—— What're you going to do?

—— I'm going to trankillize you for the full count, baby. Kay-oh. Out.

—— What is it?

—— It's a cuckoo-cocktail, son. Now come on. Easy does it.

They drove it into him. The two men stood back, panting and sweating.

It was then—on the instant, to John's surprise, long before the drug could possibly have taken effect—that he felt the ease, the relief, the cool bliss of, this time, a swift heaven riding on hell's heels.

The white one said: —— Count backwards, college boy. That'll dilly you down.

29

Minus three and counting . . . two fifty-eight, two fifty-seven, two fifty-six, two fifty-five . . .

John had the vaguest impression that he and Chum Breed were sitting side by side on straight-backed wooden chairs in a place, an enclosure, a capsule—a hospital room? a college room? What were those gyrations, convolutions, pulsations on the wall? Controls? A reserve of motive power of some sort? Candy canes, Möbius bands, Albers squares? In front of the chairs was Breed's undoubtable coffee table: on it, a little fruit, a pitcher of drinking water, the electric clock. All they would need, it seemed Breed had said.

Less than two minutes.

—— Are you go?

—— I'm go through and through. We've waited so damn long.

Where was the small glass pig-within-pig-within-pig? Would its not being on the instrument panel cause any trouble? John focused his larger misgivings on that small fear.

They were in the final minute. John became joyous at seeing the second hand of the clock wipe relentlessly, with a steady sweep, round and round, cutting off the past. He felt welling within him a lightness, a grace, a courage he hadn't known since . . . since . . .

. . . Eight, seven, six, five, four, three, two, one—*lift-off*. Whoo-oo-oo-s-s-s-s-sshh-h-h-h!

At first they hovered just off the floor in the most subtle levitation, a kind of floating on a deep-piled carpet of emotional energy; then, as the thrust of psychokinesis took more and more effect, they drifted upwards to, and then through, the ceiling (yet the op art went with them, in full flutteration, and the coffee table, and the chairs under them) and up through some slovenly idiot's room upstairs, and up through the beams of the attic and the slate roof, into the starry cavern of the eve of Rood Mass Day.

Below, John saw the lights of a town receding—a main street with the regular yellowy blobs of light thrown downward by street lamps, neon winking all along, the little white castle of an Esso station, lights in bedroom windows, car-beetles pushing their lumines-cences before them, then—the college carillon tower whited by floodlights! Were the glass bells chiming ever so faintly? On the flying coffee table the clock showed for an instant all hands standing straight up, and then the inexorable wiper moved onward into the witching hours, eating into the future.

The impression of acceleration was overwhelming, yet John felt no wind in his hair, no pressure of G's on the seat and slats of the chair; there was a constant rhythmic motion, yawing, faster and faster. They must very soon have broken through the speed of sound, yet they were bathed, too, in sound—stuttering, beating. Motion and sound were in perfect phase, and the insistent, repetitive, unwavering rhythms soon became hypnotic. On the two chairs in the night sky: Morning *raga*, cha-cha-cha, the wild beat of Welsh hymns, a voodoo *houngan* swaying to imperative drums, revivalists' cadences pounding in hysterical neck arteries, the Maulawiyah whirl, involuntary orgasmic pulsations of space itself. It seemed endless, ever-moving—and at last John fell into a state of infra-human, extrasensory ecstasy. Soaring, soaring spirit!

How long? A few moments?

Then they could see a bald mountain ahead: huge wrinkled cloudlike roundnesses of barren granite, like a naked geologic cerebellum against the dark skull of the sky.

As they came rapidly closer the terrain on the mountain could be seen to be harsh and eye-stingingly beautiful. Rock, moor, knob, vale, scarp. In the crevices there seemed to be bushy places. The stone looked as cold as the moon.

Slowing down, their flying chairs settled toward a huge primeval bowl in the mountainside, a great valley rimmed with crags like the Tetons. Their speed was spent; they floated down. They touched and left the chairs and walked.

—— Hurry (Breed said). They'll be beginning soon.

John saw that there were many, many other celebrants arriving, some settling down from the air, others already on foot. Looking up, he saw stars briefly blotted out by shapes coming in.

There was no moon, yet the rock-scape glowed. It had an ancient, sun-split, glacier-scraped look, and John had a feeling of scrambling across the most remote antiquities; he skirted a drumlin, climbed over an esker, eased along a steep scree, ducked around a huge donnick, and took the view from the crest of a kame.

A moor lay ahead, a rounded rise covered with grasses and low bushes. And on the moor, near its top, stood an outcropping, a natural rock platform. Every creature seemed to be converging on that high ground, that stone tribune.

—— We'll have to run if we want to get close.

They began to trot. John felt the lightness, the courage, that had given him such speed earlier, and his feet barely seemed to touch the ground. Nevertheless, his legs seemed thick. The path was all uphill. He developed a stitch in his side.

Others were beginning to run now—a host. Ugly people and the short-legged freaks of Breughel and Bosch. As they ran, Breed, panting, put names to some of the creatures: There were John Fian of Saltpans, Agnes Sampson, and the North Berwick witches. Those awful things? Why, lutins, poltergeists, hobhursts, dobbies, house cobolds, stable goblins. Not to be worried about. All to be thought of as in a dream. And the straightforward metamorphoses: a hare, formerly a lecher of Nîmes; a black goat, a priest-fornicator of Viareggio; a lizard, a fag from Indianapolis; moles, bats, foxes, ravens, mice, frogs, black dogs, toads, spitting cats with high backs—and there was a werewolf, a female, in a bad way with her heat.

John was not in fact the least bit troubled by this company. There was such a chatter of good fellowship all around, of anticipation, of mindless, sensual joy.

As they climbed the moor, they saw all around them in the grass and bushes broken, neglected artifacts of civilization, signs of dereliction and bad management, of laziness, forgetfulness, and incompetence. Were they abandoned vehicles? An old refrigerator, having cylindrical works on its top, lying on its side, with no door, its enamel eaten along the edges by rust. A spinning wheel with broken spokes. A battered Lambretta with no tires. A toilet fixture, its water tank smashed, the paint on its wooden oval seat curling and peeling. An ancient Hoover vacuum cleaner with a ripped dust bag. A kerosene lantern, with cracked lights of paper-thin horn, affixed to the top of a dry-rotted post. A hame, a tire, a ski, a rug, a split ironing board. The higher they climbed, the more vivid was the sense of a vast junkyard, a repository of unrealized hopes, corroded memories, ambitions flung away as absurd.

John wondered: —— Did so many who came here never go back?

At last they were standing in the murmuring assemblage not far from the flat rock at the top of the moor.

A hollow, mournful, prolonged hoot could be heard, and John saw a hairy man up on the platform holding a ram's horn to his bare behind. At that long tenor breakwind signal the crowd fell silent.

Now began a ritual, the details of which Breed explained to John. Breed! How his face had lighted up, with a pink glow of malevolence! There were swellings at each side of his forehead; he appeared to be dressed in a black cutaway coat and a crimson vest, and wore nothing from the waist down.

—— Those are the Thessalian witches setting out the Boss's pisspot, so he can make holy water. That homunculus is sweeping the platform. Sh-h-h-h! Here He comes!

Up at one end climbs Himself, with a flaming red beard, hobbling with the help of one wooden crutch.

John feels flames on his cheeks. Frank, of the beach colony! Followed by Fay, Laetitia, and Susan, who have vine leaves in their hair. All three are topless now; skirts of hanging strips of kelp. Breed says they are Himself's personal witches, and their real names are Raise-the-Wind, Over-the-Dike-with-It, and Batter-Them-Down-Maggie.

The Boss is dressed-undressed like Breed; his legs are hairy, goat-like; he has a long, unpleasant, pointed tail like a possum's.

The multitude applauds with a murmur, a sad sound of m's, a sound of something tasting good.

The Boss raises his arms and (in Frank's bold bass voice, unmistakably!) bellows an incantation, a summons:

—— *Percussimus foedus cum morte et cum inferno fecimus pactum!*

From the assemblage: —— M-m-m-m-m-m.

Then He turns His back to the crowd and relieves Himself interminably into the pot. One by one, Raise-, Over-, and Batter- lift his tail. On his bottom there is a second face, which looks astonishingly like Breed's and is, like Breed's, quick to flash ingratiating smiles.

Breed is hissing in John's ear: —— You can drink the urine of a person who has drunk the urine of a person who—to the number of five, seriatim—leading to a person who has nibbled at an *Amanita muscaria* mushroom, and still have the most exquisite hallucinations.

John shakes his head. He is impatient with Breed; he feels a whiff of strength, of something like stubbornness.

Now begin the homages. The human figures, the creatures, the shapes—all begin to file up onto the platform to kiss the nether face of Himself, who is bent over to receive the adoration of the flock. The girls hold up the possum tail.

Breed urges John to get on the line. He refuses. He absolutely refuses.

Breed pinches him, and each pinch leaves a sharp sting, like that of a sniper's dart. But John is steadfast; he feels infusing into his tissues the strength of the major walking with such integrity along the forest path at the head of the column of men.

A picnic is under way. The Mothers pass baskets. Delicious viands—m-m-m-m. A tart wine—Himself's pee? John spits it out at the thought. Nevertheless, in time, it seems to him that the food he has swallowed is having a definite aphrodisiac effect.

There is music. He sees that Susan is playing her dry guitar. Maypoles are up. Dancing has begun, and the motions become more and more abandoned.

Soon couples are peeling out and tumbling among the thrown-away possessions.

There are the Salem girls—nine-year-old Elizabeth Parris, daughter of the Parson, being fondled by a middle-aged bachelor; Abigail Williams, eleven, her cousin, in the arms of a grocer's delivery boy; sailors in shore-leave whites swarm on black Tituba and the sexually riper accusers, Mary Walcott, sixteen, Elizabeth Booth, sixteen, Susannah Sheldon, eighteen. Senator Joe McCarthy, on his knees, is committing sodomy with an incubus, croaking that he wants to rise to a point of order. A hooded Klansman is fumbling at his robes before a brown-skinned tenant woman. A suburban husband is sneaking a quick one with the wife of the chairman of the membership committee. A large number of those who cannot govern their inner selves but all too gladly band together to govern their neighbors' wills as their own proud minds dictate—censors, removers of books from library shelves, boycotters of films, writers of letters to networks, prigs, peepers, feelers, dreamers, definers and secret fracturers of Values—are diddling or being diddled by the most deviant of succubi and incubi. In the midst of the orgy Professor Gutwillig is teaching a seminar of evil spirits. Breed names the pupils: Chill, Auerhahn, Ashtoreth, Asmodeus, Megara, Krummschal, Erebus, Vitzliputzli. The nuns of Loudon are pulling their habits up over their bare legs and abdomens, bending their knees, offering their privacies, and crying out:

—— Enter here! Free gash! Uck us! *Foutez-moi!*

In the center of all this John experiences a desperate control, a raging inviolacy, a careful shuffling of the parts of the huge puzzle. He wants to start a shouting fight with Breed but feels throat-parched, inarticulate. Not that he is free of all desire. Susan, alias Batter-Them-Down-Maggie, is weaving lewdly and beckoning to him. But he feels that he is waiting to put all the diversities together into a pattern that makes more sense than he can see anywhere, anywhere.

Up on the platform Himself is strapping on a huge phallus of horn or metal, and now the Mothers come up for ceremonial coitus. Each in her turn draws in her breath hard and screams at the terrible icy coldness of his dildo.

Now John sees his own mother waiting in the line. She is just about to step up onto the platform.

John breaks away from Breed and rushes to her.

When she first sees him, she is poised, gracious, even though her hair is unkempt as a mouse nest, and there are purple bags, bruises of dissatisfaction and guilt, under her eyes.

—— Why, Johnny-cake! Darling. How wonderful to see you here.

John (horrified): —— You. What are you doing at a sabbath?

Her self-possession collapses: —— I didn't choose this. I was brought here. I was put here. You have to believe me. Darling, I didn't choose Worcester, either. I didn't want any part of that whole life. I was simply *put* there.

—— I suppose you didn't choose Father. I suppose you didn't want me.

—— I did want you. I needed you. I wanted you to save us, to save our marriage. I have a complex about having neglected you, darling. And now you've been paying me back in kind, haven't you?

—— I asked you a question. What are you doing here?

—— You never write. I don't believe you ever read my letters, you can't be reading them, because I'll ask you to do something for me and you *never* do it. I never even would have known that you'd gone skiing at Christmas— our *family* time—if you hadn't run out of money. There's just a total total total lack of communication. When you do come home you never let us know ahead of time, you just walk in the front door and all I can get out of you is a series of grunts. I don't know what to make of any part of you. What is this haircut business? I personally like your hair long, it bothers your father more than I—but what does it prove? What are you trying to prove?

—— Oh God, Mother, not *communication!* Listen, this line is moving (they are now up on the platform), you aren't going to . . . to . . . You aren't, are you, Mother?

—— You have a life of your own—you insist on it. Why shouldn't I have one of mine?

233

—— But *this*?

—— Why are you children so prudish? You give our values a big horse-laugh, you sound so cynical—but really you're a hundred times more puritanical underneath than your father and I ever were.

—— Only about things that matter. *This*? With *Him*?

—— Aren't I entitled to some kind of kicks—at long last? I've heard you talk about experiences; you want to Try Everything. What about somebody else? I spent years and years slaving for you kids, boiling the bottles in the sterilizer, fixing the formula, getting the bag ready for the diaper service. . . .

—— Oh come on, Mom, not the sacrificial bit!

—— But it's not fair, son. You accuse us of being hypocritical. You always gripe about the gap between moral pretensions and actual performance. Did you ever think of the example *you* set *us*? That girl—that woman you brought home. She had a dreadful purple ointment. I looked in her suitcase. I had to find out something about her somehow. It said on the label: *Dr. Savon. Apply three times daily and at bedtime. If bedtime is more than three times daily, apply anyway.*

—— But Mom, Mom! This is different.

—— How different? Because it's another generation? Because every woman over twenty-five years of age is a witch?

Something strange is happening to John. Always in the past, when he has become locked in a struggle with his mother, he has seemed able to put her in the wrong at first, but she has always seemed gradually to straighten up, to muster color in her cheeks, to begin to purr; the more he has placed her in a disadvantageous light, the more she has glowed—until, in the end, she has invaria-

234

bly emerged wholly composed, in bloom, dead right. And at the end, every time, victorious to the point of *noblesse oblige*. She has been able to give him a pat on the head, a kiss on the brow. But now, this time, John has begun to feel this very process taking place in himself. The knot in his chest is dissolving into a warm fluid of trust—self-trust, at the beginning. His new confidence has its cruel edge, at first. He cannot help enjoying this experience of invulnerability a little too much.

—— But listen to those women scream, Mother.

A look of distress comes into her eyes. He exults in it.

She: —— It's too late.

—— What you mean is, you really want to scream.

—— No! No! What I really want is to sit down and talk with you. This is the best talk we've had in such a long time.

There were now only three women in the line ahead of John's mother.

—— Mom, you've really got to make up your mind.

—— Darling (suddenly soft, yielding), you decide for me.

—— I won't let you. I won't let this happen.

—— Yes! Yes!

But he cannot make out what the yeses mean. Do they mean yes, she wants him to prevent this? Or yes, she wants this to happen? Her face does not give the answer, even though it is now completely passive, feminine, full of the energy-charged beauty of her youth: frightened, expectant.

John, flooded with trust and a major's integrity, steps close to her and gently takes her arm.

But now Breed is pushing between them—his face crimson as his waistcoat.

John reacts strongly: —— Get away from me, you parasite. You virus.

Breed does turn away, and, as he has done once before, he rather grandly snaps finger off thumb. The gesture is in the direction of Professor Gutwillig's seminar. Gutwillig nods, snaps his own fingers. Several of the vile students jump up. They rush to the platform and two of them, Erebus and Ashtoreth, who are respectively black and white, grab John and pull him down off the raised rock.

John's mother tries to plunge after them, but Vitzliputzli and Asmodeus seize her, and they drag her to Himself, who is now free and waiting. Mrs. Fist has begun to cry out even before being cold-cocked. The two big fellows hold her down. The Boss descends on her.

She begins to scream: —— Help! Help! Rape! Somebody help me! I'm being raped!

There is a sound of windows being raised all along a city block. Silent heads appear in the nonexistent windows. The screaming grows ever more shrill. Nobody does anything.

30

THE first John knew was that he had a sore head. He tried to move. He ached all over. He lay supine, thinking: —— This has happened before.

But then he heard screaming; that was something new.

He moved his palm. Carpet—he was on a floor. He was sandpaper-stiff at every juncture of gristle and bone, but he managed to raise his throbbing head.

He saw a wall; spirals, curves, squares. Quickly he closed his eyes and lowered his head again. The screaming did not end.

Then, opening his eyes once more, he rose to his knees and crawled to the window. Outside: such brilliance! A brilliant day in May. On a blossoming branch of a crab-apple tree below (with sudden midday clarity the name of the variety came to him, *Malus halliana parkmani*, and he experienced, on remembering this profitless fact his father had taught him, a weak pulsing of that dimly remembered new awareness—trust, a fragile belief in something he would henceforth have to regard as the one and only John Fist)—down on that branch, screaming its head off, a baby bluejay perched, almost as big as an adult bird, ragged-feathered, pure azure and white against the red of the blooms, flecks of sky and curtain side by side in the tree.

A parent bird came and gagged its child's shrilling throat with a fat caterpillar. After a gulp the screaming at once resumed.

John stood up, swayed. Where was Breed? John went out onto the stair landing and into the bathroom and saw, passing the mirrors, that his face was gray and had several days' growth of beard and a drifter's empty stare. He went in the can and threw up.

Then he jounced downstairs on unsteady legs, and he walked with growing confidence across the campus, under elm trees which were fountains of Robin Hood green, where goldfinches and redstarts flashed, and he climbed to his own room and found, thank goodness (or badness?), that Flack was out. He shaved, and took an endless shower in steaming jets of water, and put on laundered linens, and then he went to Emil's and gorged: a tall juice, squeezed as he watched, and three eggs scrambled, and grainy Canadian bacon, and sweet rolls studded with currants, and four cups of Emil's coffee that had a kick like a sixteen-gauge shotgun.

After that he began to walk around in the sparkling day, seeing chimneys, license plates, flicking skirt hems, doorbell buttons, human fingers, parking meters, high heels . . .

Two days passed—long sleeping and lazy reading. Then he came in from a stroll late in the afternoon and found a note on his desk.

> *Where you been keeping y'rself? Whyn't you drop over?* *Chum*

For reasons not quite clear to him, John decided to go to see Breed very early in the morning two days later. He knew it was a Tuesday, and he remembered, on his way to Breed's room, that old Oval Ears lectured at ten-ten on Tuesdays.

Breed was barely up; sharp Breed in a T-shirt and rumpled pajama bottoms, unshaven, lolling in his easy chair with bleary eyes, gathering strength to dress. His eyebrows shot up at the sight of John.

—— Early bird. Been to matins?

—— You wrote me a note.

—— So formal so early.

—— What did you want?

Breed sat up straight and looked hard at John.

—— Hiddledy-diddledy. You sound as if you'd had a big fat breakfast.

John did not answer but dared now to look at the op art. The canes were still, the squares serene. He looked back at Breed, who said:

—— I don't know whether you've been counting, but our twenty-six weeks are going to be up on Friday. I wanted to discuss the renewal with you.

John thought for a moment his knees were going to give way. He concentrated, without looking at it, on a memory of the Albers painting, steady this morning, pale on pale on pale. Then in a hesitant voice he said:

—— I need to ask you a couple of questions.

—— Sure.

—— First of all, time has gotten mixed up in my mind, the way you said it would. Was the night we went to Cruel Creek, when I made the climb—was that before or after you gave me the LSD?

For a moment Breed looked puzzled, as if he had never been to, or even heard of, any such place as Cruel Creek. Then quickly, with a triumphant spark in his eye, he said:

—— What climb? What are you talking about?

—— Up those balconies! You know what I mean.

—— You've lost me, son.

—— Another thing, how did we get to—

But John broke off, shaking his head, as if to clear it. That momentary look of puzzlement on Breed's face! Followed by such a look of gloating! How could one trust his answers? After a long pause John said:

—— Let me tell you about an experience I had yesterday. I was walking along Painter Street—when was it?—yes, it was yesterday—I thought I might walk down and have a look at the Cruel Creek district again, I don't know exactly why. Anyway, I was just about to turn into Ash Street, when I saw a dame—you remember it was windy but nice yesterday, those little good-weather clouds going over?—and just as I began to pay attention to this girl she came out from under a cloud. I mean the shadow of a cloud moved off her. She came out in full sunshine. I sort of jumped because she was so . . . so real. Her dress blowing against her . . . And then she began walking toward me and then she was running, sort of holding her hands up like this, as if she wanted to give me something. And then, jeepers, I really flipped, because it was Margaret—the girl you picked up for me, the one I took to the motel. And listen, she just plowed into me and threw her arms around me. And she was sobbing. When she could finally string two words together, her face was looking up at me with her cheeks wet and she asked why had I dropped her. What had she done? She'd thought she was going to die missing me. . . . I mean right in the street, guys going by. . . . It made me feel as if I'd been to the goddam moon. It also made me feel great, I may as well say it. I hadn't felt so good since—

John abruptly stopped, biting his tongue to keep it from saying: —— since climbing up those tenement balconies.

Breed: —— What crap! You're making up every stupid word of it.

Now John felt a fiery hot blush spread on his face and neck.

—— I'm not going to renew. . . .

That short declaration drove the scorn from Breed's face and voice, and now he spoke softly, solicitously:

—— Why not?

—— Because I can't go on living in a world that's on a knife-edge between hallucination and objective truth.

—— Sentimentality can never be the truth.

—— Who said I wanted sentimentality?

—— That lousy experience you dreamed up yesterday with Margaret. . . .

—— But that wasn't an *experience;* you just said it yourself—that I dreamed it up. You haven't given me *experiences.* I can't live with frenzy, visions, stupor, hangovers—and finally a tremor, a dragging foot as I walk. You sold me a bill of goods. You sold me illusions. I prefer the real world, crummy as it is.

—— Who's to say what's real? Do you know what's real?

TOO FAR TO WALK

——— I don't know for sure, but I think reality has
something to do with friction—in all senses—between
human beings, and what you put me through was a series
of flights into myself, away from other people, the opposite of that friction. I can't deny there were marvelous
moments—

——— Marvelous moments! And do you think you
could understand this little bit that you've begun to understand now, about yourself, and about what you think
reality may be, if it hadn't been for those flights into
yourself, as you call them?

——— I don't know the answer to that. Maybe not. But
I know that I didn't get what I thought I was bargaining
for—I didn't get what *I* think of as breakthroughs:
ecstasies, theophanies, glimpses of the meaning of life.
You promised me a lot, Chum. Too much.

——— What makes you think the other way will lead
to anything but premature aging, suburban fatuousness,
decay, sloppy drinking, wife-swapping, degradation? At
the very least, dullness. Dullness and dullness.

——— Your promises were bait. I think you're a
breaker, you're only interested in breaking people, cor-
rupting them, and finally destroying them. Isn't that so? I
feel as if I've got to save myself while I can.

——— For what? For a dull, stupid, conforming,
middle-class life?

——— For life, anyway. For that friction I was talking
about. I'd rather grope and blunder and fail than exist in
this vacuum of queer dreams.

John saw that Breed was now the one whose face
was burning; Breed was growing angry:

——— Dreams? Think of the vividness with which
you've been seeing things. You'll be as blind as a mole
again in a week. You told me at the outset, before we

made the deal, that what you wanted was sharpened perceptions—you wanted an *intensity* in your life that hadn't been there. Haven't I given you that?

—— But all that was artificial, that's my real complaint. I've come to see that there can't be any shortcut to those breakthroughs I yearn for. You can't imbibe them, or smoke them, or take them intravenously, or get them by crossing your legs and breathing deeply for twenty minutes. I guess you just have to work like hell for them, grub for them with the other grubs, and maybe you won't have them even then. But they aren't worth having any other way. Not your way. I don't want them your way.

—— What makes you so sure you can take care of yourself any more?

—— I'm not . . . sure. I'm not at all sure. I don't really know whether I can make it at all, especially here at college. . . . I'm so far behind.

—— It'll all be flat. Boring, boring, boring.

Breed began to laugh, and suddenly John felt frightened. John looked at the clock. Twenty minutes to ten. The second hand, cold black metal, was wiping, wiping.

—— I have to go to a class.

At that Breed's laughter grew into a cascade of ridicule. John turned and left. As he went down the stairwell he heard the pealing of Breed's voice; with his rattled senses he seemed to feel the laughter swirling around him, trying to hold him, pinching him with tiny sniper stings. John began to run down the steps.

Outside, the air was bland. He inhaled deeply, held his breath, and let it go in a long sigh. He did suddenly feel unspeakably dull.

He walked to the glass phone booth at the corner of Planique and Elm. He dropped in a dime, dialed O, gave a number.

—— Hello.

John almost laughed out loud at the relief he felt at the sound of his father's voice.

—— Hey, Dad. What're you doing home?

—— I'm just leaving for the office now. Slept a little late. What are *you* doing up so early?

—— Excuse the collect call, I didn't seem to have any change.

—— That was a joke about being up early. You know that, don't you?

—— Mom home?

—— Hold on.

Was that an echo of Breed's laughter even here in the public booth?

—— What's the matter, son, has something happened? Are you all right?

—— I just wondered. I was thinking maybe next weekend . . .

—— You *mean*—

—— Oh, Mom, for God's sake don't *jump* at me that way.

Silence.

John: —— What've you done, swallowed the whole damn telephone?

—— Will you be bringing a . . . a person with you?

—— I don't know. (John felt a heavy weight of doubt. His shoulders shook; he shuddered with what his mother had used to call, when he was small, a pee chill.) I might. I'm not really sure I can come at all.

—— Then why call?

—— If I do bring someone, it'll be a different one.

—— I should hope so.

—— You sound pretty hospitable. Brother.

—— Have you decided about next year?

—— It might be the one I wrote about.

—— What?

—— The girl I wrote about maybe bringing her home. I don't know if she'd want to now.

—— What about next year? Have you decided?

—— Not really.

—— Thank *goodness*. What a relief!

—— What do you mean?

—— I mean you haven't done anything . . . unrealistic. We were so concerned.

—— Oh, I'm a red-hot not-doer. . . .

When at the end he hung up, he felt confused, puzzled, yet somehow less heavy-headed than before.

Then it struck him that it would be an O.K. morning to walk to Humblesmith, and he turned northward.

At one point on the way he stopped; his eyes were caught by the winged euonymus, its leaves, at this season, a thin feathery shimmer of greens. He stood there, asking himself: How far would be too far to walk on this particular day?

Soon: *Clackertavoom.* The metal door handle at Humblesmith.

John took a seat about halfway down the amphitheater.

The shock of shampooed white. The huge eyes.

John had just begun to wonder what he was doing sitting there when old Oval Ears started in:

—— Gentlemen. My theme this morning is classical passion. It may surprise you to hear me begin by quoting a Latin, rather than a Greek, poet. Catullus is distinguished by the lightning stroke. Hear this:

Odi et amo. Quare id faciam, fortasse requiris.
Nescio, sed fieri sentio et excrucior.

Those first words! *Oh-di et ah-mo*. Twenty-five years ago I would not have insulted my students by translating. Such is the state of learning today that I must, I know, besmirch this beginning of one of the greatest of love lyrics by eking it out for you in our poor monosyllables:

I hate and love. You ask how that can be?
I know not, but I feel the agony.

A NOTE

ABOUT THE AUTHOR

JOHN HERSEY was born in Tientsin, China, in 1914, and lived there until 1925, when his family returned to the United States. He was graduated from Yale in 1936 and attended Clare College, Cambridge University, for a year. He was private secretary to Sinclair Lewis during a subsequent summer and then worked as a journalist and war correspondent. His first novel, *A Bell for Adano*, won the Pulitzer Prize in 1945, and the next year he wrote *Hiroshima*, an account of the first atomic bombing. Since 1947 he has devoted his time mainly to fiction and has published *The Wall* (1950), *The Marmot Drive* (1953), *A Single Pebble* (1956), *The War Lover* (1959), *The Child Buyer* (1960), and *White Lotus* (1964). Mr. Hersey completed the writing of *Too Far to Walk* just before he took up his current post as Master of Pierson College at Yale.

January 1966

A NOTE ON THE TYPE

The text of this book was set in a typeface called Primer, designed by Rudolph Ruzicka for the Mergenthaler Linotype Company and first made available in 1949. Primer, a modified modern face based on Century Expanded, has the virtue of great legibility and was designed especially for today's methods of composition and printing.

Primer is Ruzicka's third typeface. In 1940 he designed Fairfield, and in 1947 Fairfield Medium, both for the Mergenthaler Linotype Company.

Ruzicka was born in Bohemia in 1883 and came to the United States at the age of eleven. He attended public schools in Chicago and later the Chicago Art Institute. During his long career he has been a wood engraver, etcher, cartographer, and book designer. For many years he was associated with Daniel Berkeley Updike and produced the annual keepsakes for The Merrymount Press from 1911 until 1941.

Ruzicka has been honored by many distinguished organizations, and in 1936 he was awarded the gold medal of the American Institute of Graphic Arts. From his home in New Hampshire, Ruzicka continues to be active in the graphic arts.

Composed, printed, and bound by
THE HADDON CRAFTSMEN, INC., SCRANTON, PA.
Binding Design by Muriel Nasser.

C2

Hersey
Too far to walk